A NEW WAY TO KNOW

JEREMY D SCHOLZ

Cover by getcovers.com

For information or permission requests, please contact: Jeremy D Scholz

https://jeremydscholz.com/

moxiemagicbooks@gmail.com

ISBN: 979-8-9994313-8-7 (Hardback)

ISBN: 979-8-9994313-9-4 (Paperback)

Printed in the United States of America

First Edition

A New Way to Know

by Jeremy D Scholz

FOREWORD

I have always felt a clear account of Francis Bacon's life and his formative years was long overdue, so I was delighted when approached by author and educator Jeremy D Sholz to read his manuscript of A New Way to Know, a historical novel aimed at middle-grade readers. The 2026 publication is particularly appropriate as it coincides with the Bacon 400 commemorations to celebrate 400 years since Bacon's death.

Scholz spent 25 years as a science teacher and has been honoured as County Teacher of the Year, a fact that did not surprise me at all. He is clearly a writer who still retains a child-like wonder about the world around him and a very engaging and direct way of communicating it. Of boy Francis he notes, "Knowledge, he realized, was like planting seeds. You buried a question in the soil, watered it with effort, and waited for truth to push its way into the light. Sometimes slowly. Sometimes unexpectedly. But always honestly."

A New Way to Know may be aimed at children aged 8-12, but its vivid descriptions, wealth of information, and heart-warming tone make it appealing to readers of all ages. Scholz skillfully brings Bacon's voice and character to life, allowing readers to experience the world through the eyes of a relentlessly curious and passionate young boy on a magnificent mission. "Francis watched everything. Listened to everything. Noted everything. It was as if he were made of magnifying glass, brightening the smallest details, even the ones nobody else thought mattered."

I have been a Baconian for over 35 years, drawn to his remarkable achievements, vast legacy and, above all, his compassion and drive to improve humanity, even at great personal cost. In this book, Bacon's sacrifices and emotional challenges are handled thoughtfully, reminding us that life can hand out difficult lessons, especially when 'truth' is the guiding principle.

The terms genius and rebel are too quickly and randomly applied these days, but with Francis Bacon both are appropriate. He was always way ahead of his time and often misunderstood. "He wasn't trying to be rebellious. He simply believed there must be a more reliable way to understand the world. Books held wisdom. Yes. But nature held evidence."

A New Way to Know is an empowering and inspirational read and will clearly speak to young readers of a world where all things are possible. For adults, it provides a powerful re-examination of Bacon's life and legacy and serves as a catalyst to perhaps recapture the wonder and hope of our youth.

2026

Sally Gibbins, Principal
The Francis Bacon Society

FRANCIS BACON, VISCOUNT ST ALBANS. LINE ENGRAVING

1

CURIOUS KID, COMPLICATED COURT

The palace of Queen Elizabeth I was not built for quiet children, or curious ones.

It was built for noise. Color. Ceremony. For the flash of silk sleeves and the scrape of polished boots. For the rustle of papers carried by frantic secretaries and the booming laughter of nobles who enjoyed hearing the sound of their own voices.

Young Francis Bacon tried to keep up with it all, walking a few steps behind his mother as she glided through the halls with the confidence of someone who understood exactly how the world worked.

Francis, on the other hand, understood exactly how the world didn't work. Which was why he had so many questions.

"Walk faster," his mother murmured, not looking back.

"Yes, Mother."

Francis hurried, nearly dropping the quill he kept tucked behind his ear. He carried his little travel notebook under one arm, tightly pressed to his side so it wouldn't fall. Most boys his age kept toys in their pockets.

Francis kept asking questions. They swarmed inside his mind like bees, constantly buzzing. Whenever he tried to think about anything else — his lessons, the Queen's rules, his mother's instructions — the questions pushed forward again.

Why does the scent of beeswax candles change when they melt? How does one person's voice fill an entire hall while another's barely reaches across a table?

Why do nobles walk as if they're floating while guards walk as if they're stomping?

"Francis," his mother said sharply, "stop staring at the ceiling."

Francis lowered his gaze. "Sorry."

He had been looking at the torches, wondering why the flames leaned toward the draft near the window. He should have been looking straight ahead, following his mother to the waiting chamber.

They were visiting court today, something Lady Bacon considered both an honor and a responsibility. Francis considered it a maze of distractions.

The halls stretched endlessly, lined with portraits of stern-faced ancestors who looked like they disapproved of everything the living were doing. Servants hurried past carrying trays. Courtiers lounged in clusters, whispering secrets and gossip. The Queen's ladies-in-waiting swept by in gowns that rustled like leaves in a breeze.

Francis watched everything. Listened to everything. Noted everything.

It was as if he were made of magnifying glass, brightening the smallest details, even the ones nobody else thought mattered. And in this palace, there were many details.

As they entered the outer hall, Francis's senses overwhelmed him. The court was like a painting come to life; everywhere he looked, colors leapt out.

A nobleman's emerald doublet embroidered with gold thread. A woman's gown of deep crimson velvet. Ribbons, feathers, jewels, polished steel, brocade shoes, and lace so fine it looked like breath. But beneath all that color, the mood felt tense, as if everyone was performing on a stage. *There was enough glitter to blind you,* Francis thought, *but only if you didn't look too closely.*

He wrote in his notebook: Court = a theater where everyone pretends they know everything.

He snapped it shut as his mother gave him a warning glance.

"Francis," she whispered, "do not take out that notebook in front of the Queen."

"I wasn't going to," he whispered back. He absolutely was.

While Lady Bacon greeted another noblewoman, Francis wandered a few steps away, drawn toward the tall stained-glass window that caught the sunlight in a dazzling rainbow. Red and blue light shimmered across the stone floor like spilled paint.

Francis knelt to touch the patches of color, fascinated. He also noted a raindrop and the way it moved down the glass. *How could colored glass make colored light? Was the light inside the glass?*

Or did the sun do something to it? And why did different colors bend in different directions? Why did the drop not move straight down?

He reached into his pocket for the notebook, forgetting the warning.

"What are you doing?" came a stern voice behind him.

Francis jumped to his feet, heart pounding. A tall guard stood there, wearing the Queen's colors and a frown that looked like it hadn't relaxed in twenty years.

"I...I was looking at the light," Francis stammered.

"The light?" the guard repeated slowly.

"Yes," Francis said. "Because—look—when the sun hits the glass, the colors spread across the floor, and I think..."

"No touching the stones," the guard barked. "No kneeling in the way of foot traffic. And absolutely no scribbling on the palace floor."

"I wasn't scribbling on the..."

"Back to your mother," the guard ordered.

Francis trudged back, cheeks burning. His mother was speaking with a noblewoman in a beaded hood. Their conversation stopped the moment they saw him.

"What did you do?" Lady Bacon asked.

"Observed," Francis muttered.

Anthony, the older brother, who had arrived earlier, now approached with a smirk and clapped him on the shoulder. "Ah. Your first crime."

"It wasn't a crime," Francis said. "I was looking at how light..."

His mother interrupted. "Francis, curiosity is a wonderful trait, but there is a time and place."

"When is it the time for questions?" Francis asked earnestly.

Lady Bacon hesitated.

Anthony supplied dryly, "Any other time, but not here, not now."

They reentered the inner hall, which the queen often passed through. In here, people held themselves a little taller and spoke in a reverent hush, each one trying to appear far more important than they actually felt.

Francis tugged at his mother's sleeve. "Why does everyone act differently here?"

"It is the royal court," Lady Bacon said. "Every gesture matters. Every word carries weight."

Francis frowned. "But why? Shouldn't truth matter more than gestures?"

Lady Bacon gave him a long, slow look. "Not always."

He added that sentence to the growing list of things that didn't make sense. But he also understood something important: The court was a ladder. And everyone was trying to climb it. Your clothes mattered. Your connections mattered. Your rank mattered. Your words mattered only if someone powerful wanted to hear them.

Francis didn't like ladders. He preferred ground-level things like: plants, puddles, and questions.

Still, today he was expected to be on his best behavior. So he folded his hands, stood up straight, and tried to keep his thoughts quiet. He tried, but his curiosity wasn't something he could switch off.

A trumpet sounded. Conversations broke off mid-sentence. Francis felt the air sharpen as Queen Elizabeth I entered the gallery, surrounded by ladies like a wave of color around a bright, commanding sun. Her gown glittered with jewels. Her ruff framed her pale face like the petals of a rare flower. Her hair, bright and curled, shimmered in the light.

Francis tried not to stare. He failed.

She moved with such controlled grace that Francis wondered: How does someone learn to walk like that? Is it balance? Practice? Or simply confidence? He wanted to ask. He did not.

As the queen passed, the courtiers bowed deeply. Francis bowed too, awkwardly, and a little too quickly. His mother nudged his shoulder to straighten him.

Elizabeth's gaze swept the room — sharp, perceptive, missing nothing. When her eyes brushed past Francis, he felt a jolt of fear mixed with fascination. What did she know? What did she see? What questions did she carry? Did she ever have time for them?

After the Queen disappeared into her private chambers, the court slowly relaxed. Francis exhaled, heart still fluttering.

Anthony leaned close. "You didn't faint. That's a good sign."

"I wasn't going to faint," Francis said.

"You looked like you might."

"I was thinking," Francis replied.

"That's even worse," Anthony teased. "Don't do too much of that here."

Francis frowned. "Where can I think, then?"

Anthony smiled softly. "Anywhere. Just... not right in the Queen's path."

Francis wasn't satisfied with that answer, but he let it go. Instead, he watched the courtiers, the flutter of fans, the tilt of heads, the way men bowed too low or too little.

He noticed all the contradictions. People smiled while hiding jealousy. They praised while plotting. They listened while pretending not to. *If the court was a machine,* Francis thought, *it was a machine powered by secrets instead of gears.*

He wrote in his notebook: *The world is complicated.*

People pretend truth instead of finding it.

That felt important. He underlined it twice.

As they prepared to leave, Francis paused at the doorway and looked back at the bustling room. So many voices. So many rules. So many ideas were repeated because they were old, not because they were true. Yet in all that chaos, Francis felt excitement bubbling inside him like a kettle beginning to boil. If the world was as complicated as court, if people accepted things without questioning them, then maybe there was room for someone willing to search for truth. Someone who saw details others ignored. Someone who asked the questions others weren't brave enough to ask. Maybe... someone like him.

His brother Anthony waved from the hallway. "Francis! Are you coming?"

Francis closed his notebook, tucked it under his arm, and

followed, but as he walked out of the palace, he felt a spark inside him — small, bright, undeniable. Curiosity. The same curiosity that had gotten him scolded today. The same curiosity that made adults sigh and guards frown, but Francis sensed somehow that curiosity wasn't a flaw. It was a beginning. And he was just getting started.

2

THE WORLD ISN'T
WHAT THEY SAY IT IS

The classroom at Trinity College at Cambridge University smelled faintly of chalk dust, damp stone, and old arguments. Francis Bacon sat straight-backed on a wooden bench, hands folded neatly, quill ready, eyes alert. He liked learning, truly liked it, but he had begun noticing something recently: learning and thinking were not always the same thing.

Today's lesson was taught by John Whitgift, a man who believed the world had reached perfection in the past and had been falling apart ever since. His beard seemed older than some of the ideas he taught.

"Now," Master Whitgift said, pacing in front of the narrow window, "as you all know, Aristotle explained the nature of everything. And since Aristotle's logic is perfect, we accept it. Repeat after me: The world is composed of four elements."

A chorus of voices chimed dutifully: "Earth, air, fire, water."

Francis said the words too, though without enthusiasm.

Master Whitgift nodded approvingly. "Yes. These four elements make up the world. They are fixed. Eternal. Unchanging."

Francis frowned ever so slightly. *Unchanging?*

Tell that to the frozen puddle Francis had seen melt in the sun that very morning. Or to the candle that burned down to nothing but wax drips. Or to the peach he'd left on the windowsill that had somehow turned into a fuzz-covered disaster.

He raised his hand.

Master Whitgift sighed before even calling on him. "Yes, young Bacon?"

Francis chose his words carefully. "If the world is unchanging, sir, how does ice melt? Or fruit rot?"

Master Whitgift waved a dismissive hand. "Those are trivial transformations. Surface-level. The underlying essence does not change. Aristotle tells us this."

"But..." Francis began.

"No buts, Master Bacon. Memorize. Don't question."

Francis pressed his lips together. Around him, the other boys smirked or rolled their eyes. Everyone knew that questioning Master Whitgift was like knocking on a sealed door; nothing ever opened.

Still, Francis couldn't help it. Questions crowded his mind the way ivy crowded the old stone walls outside. *Why didn't the explanations match what he saw? Why did people repeat ideas without checking them? Why did tradition outrank observation?*

Francis tried to refocus as Master Whitgift launched into another recitation, this one about how heavier objects fell faster, another teaching attributed to Aristotle.

"Take this down," Whitgift ordered. "A stone falls more swiftly than a feather because its nature seeks the ground."

Francis scribbled the words, but not because he accepted them. He wrote them the way an investigator writes down suspicious statements, to examine later.

Francis already knew something Aristotle didn't: Feathers

got tossed about by air, not because they "didn't want" to fall. He'd seen it himself.

The rest of the lesson was the same: memorize, repeat, accept. Books were read aloud as if they were sacred relics. Students copied diagrams older than the building itself. No one asked why things worked the way they did. No one tested anything. Knowledge in Master Whitgift's classroom was a museum — dusty, admired, untouched.

When the bell finally rang, the boys leapt up with relief, eager to escape into the courtyard. Francis moved slower, his head still buzzing with unanswered questions.

Anthony waited for him at the door, arms crossed. "Another thrilling adventure in the land of recitation?"

Francis gave a weak smile. "He said heavier objects fall faster."

Anthony snorted. "Next he'll tell us the sun moves around the earth."

"He already did," Francis said.

Anthony groaned. "The world is doomed."

"Not doomed," Francis said softly. "Just... mistaken."

They walked together out of the room, the large wooden door closing behind them with a heavy thud. Francis felt the weight of it. A door between what was taught and what was true.

After lunch, Francis wandered into the gardens behind the inn, notebook in hand. The air smelled of damp soil and early blossoms. A thin thread of sunlight wound through the branches overhead.

He crouched near a patch of grass and plucked a fallen feather. Holding it between his fingers, he studied its delicate form. He dropped it. It fluttered, drifted, and finally landed. Then, he picked up a small pebble and dropped it beside the feather. The pebble plunged straight to the ground. Francis felt a spark in his chest, confirmation. Evidence. Proof that matched his observation, not what was written in a book by someone important.

He opened his notebook. It was new. The leather still stiff, the pages blank except for his name on the inside cover.

He turned to the first page and wrote carefully at the top: Things That Don't Make Sense

Then underneath:

1. Master Whitgift says heavier objects fall faster.
2. → But a feather and a pebble fall differently because of the air, not because they "want" to fall.
3. Aristotle says the four elements never change.
4. → But ice melts. Candles burn. Fruit rots.
5. Some teachers say the truth cannot be questioned.
   → But if we don't question, how do we learn anything new?

Francis looked at the list. This notebook — this small, secret thing — felt alive, filled with possibility. A place where he could write what others refused to see. It was a symbol of a different kind of learning. Not obedience. Not repetition. Discovery. As Francis wrote, a breeze fluttered the pages.

Anthony wandered over, hands stuffed in his pockets. "You're writing again? Didn't we just escape from hours of that?"

Francis shook his head. "This is different."

Anthony raised an eyebrow. "How?"

Francis tapped the notebook. "This is for me, not because I'm told."

Anthony sat beside him on the grass. "So, what's in it?"

Francis hesitated, then said, "I'm keeping track of everything that doesn't fit. Everything that might be wrong."

Anthony blinked. "That's going to be a long list."

Francis smiled faintly. "I hope so."

He held the notebook gently, almost reverently. Each page felt like soil waiting for a seed. A place where questions could grow roots. A place that might someday grow into something revolutionary.

Classes continued the same way over the next week — recitations of old authorities, diagrams copied without thought. The medieval method of education ruled: memorize the master, trust tradition, accept the past as perfect.

But Francis was changing. He found himself looking for cracks in what he had been taught.

One day Whitgift lectured about the heavens. "The stars," he declared, "are fixed in perfect spheres. They never change. Never move."

The next night, Francis stared out of his window and watched a star appear to shift position, just a little, as the hours passed.

He opened his notebook.

1. Aristotle says the stars never move. → But they rise
   and fall across the sky.

He wrote late into the night, the candles guttering low. He didn't know it yet, but he was beginning to think like the new scholars of the Renaissance, the ones who believed the world should be studied through sight, not superstition; observation, not obedience.

He was stepping out of the medieval world and into a new one.

One morning, as Master Whitgift lectured on how the human body worked, "Four humors, always perfectly balanced unless upset by sinful behavior," he insisted.

Francis whispered to the boy next to him: "But if the humors are balanced in everyone, why do different people react differently to illness?"

The boy looked at him as though Francis had just questioned the existence of the sky. "Because the book says so," he whispered back.

"That doesn't make sense," Francis murmured.

The boy shrugged. "Doesn't have to."

Francis sat back, troubled. *Doesn't have to.* That was the problem. People were content with explanations that didn't match reality simply because someone older or ancient had declared them true.

He felt something shift inside him, small but irreversible. The world was not what they said it was.

And he wanted, needed, to understand it for himself.

That afternoon, Francis returned to the garden. The sunlight filtered gently through the pear tree's branches, warming the surrounding ground. The earth smelled of growth.

He took out his notebook again. This time, instead of listing what didn't make sense, he wrote:

If the world in books disagrees with the world before my eyes, I will trust my eyes.

He underlined it twice. Then he added: *Truth can never be reached by just listening to the voice of an authority.*

Francis closed the notebook, holding it tightly to his chest. It was small. It was his secret. It would get him in trouble someday. But it was his first step toward the truth. Real truth, not recited truth. And as he stood and brushed grass from his cloak, he felt something unexpected. Not fear. Not confusion. Hope. Because for the first time in his life, Francis Bacon wasn't just learning. He was beginning to think.

3

A SUDDEN CHANGE

On the night Francis Bacon's childhood ended, he was far from England.

He slept in a narrow bed in a cold French lodging, the kind arranged quickly for men on royal errands, clean enough, forgettable, meant to be temporary. The fire in the hearth had burned low. Outside, the wind worried at the shutters like a restless thought. Francis dreamed.

In the dream, his country home stood silent beneath a dreary sky. Black cloth hung from every window, heavy and unmoving, as if the house itself were in mourning. No voice echoed in the halls. No servants moved through the rooms. Even the birds were absent. He walked toward the door, each step slower than the last, knowing—without knowing why — that he should not go inside.

When he reached for the handle, his hand passed through it, as though the house was already no longer solid.

Francis woke with a sharp intake of breath. The room was dark. The fire had died. His heart thudded painfully against his ribs, not from fear exactly, but from recognition. The dream clung to him with unnatural weight. This was not imagination. It was a certainty. Something dreadful had happened.

He sat up slowly, pressing his palm against his chest as if to steady the knowledge that had arrived fully formed, without words. He had experienced worry before, about politics, about favor, about money, but this was different.

Inevitably, the knock came. Measured. Formal. Inevitable. A messenger stood in the corridor, hat clutched low, eyes trained carefully away from Francis's face. He bowed and extended a sealed letter bearing an English mark. Francis did not open it immediately. He already knew. Still, his fingers trembled as he broke the seal. The words swam briefly before settling into meaning. Sir Nicholas Bacon, Lord Keeper of the Great Seal of England, is dead.

For a moment, Francis could not breathe.

The mission, the Queen's business, the language, the schedules—all of it fell away. The room felt suddenly too small, as if the walls had drawn closer. His father had been a constant presence in the world: authority made flesh, reason given a voice. And now that presence was simply... absent.

Francis lowered himself back onto the bed, the letter crumpling slightly in his grasp. His mind raced ahead, cruelly efficient, cataloging consequences before his heart could catch up. Inheritance. Position. Protection. Guidance. And beneath it all, something more fragile and more terrible: he would never again hear his father's voice. Never again receive a correction or quiet approval. Never again measure himself against that steady, formidable example.

Tears came then, silent and unrestrained, streaking down his face as he bent forward, clutching the letter to his chest. He had crossed a threshold in the night, without ceremony, without farewell. Childhood had ended not with a sound, but with absence.

When Francis finally rose to dress, his hands were steadier than he felt. There would be duties now. Letters to send. Arrangements to make. A return to England he was no longer prepared for.

But something fundamental had shifted. The world had changed.

And Francis Bacon, standing alone in a foreign country with grief heavy in his lungs, understood with sudden, painful clarity that whatever came next, whatever he became, would be built without his father standing behind him.

Sir Nicholas had been a presence that filled rooms. Now, it was his absence that filled them instead.

The funeral occurred before Francis' return, and now he was feeling quite low. Anthony found Francis sitting on the cold stone steps of their residence. Anthony sat beside him. For a long time, neither spoke.

Finally, Francis whispered, "Everything feels different."

Anthony's voice was low. "It is."

Francis pulled his knees close. "I knew Father was important. But I didn't realize how much depended on him until now."

Anthony nodded slowly. "We're about to learn."

Later, Francis learned the truth in the most practical, painful way possible. He, Anthony, and their mother sat at a long table covered with papers. Two legal clerks stood across from them, explaining matters of inheritance.

Sir Nicholas had been a wealthy man. But wealth did not mean what Francis assumed. Much of it belonged to the Crown. Another portion was tied up in land, leases, and promises made to the older sons from his first marriage.

"What does this mean for us?" Anthony asked, his brows knotted.

The clerk cleared his throat. "It means, Master Bacon, that the younger sons," he glanced at Francis, "receive much less than the elder."

"How much less?" Anthony pressed.

The clerk avoided Francis's eyes.

Lady Bacon stiffened. "Say it plainly."

"As it stands," the clerk said carefully, "there are... limited funds remaining for Master Francis."

Francis felt something hollow open inside him.

He hadn't expected riches, but he hadn't expected nothing.

He swallowed. "So I must earn my own way?"

The clerk gave a sympathetic half-bow. "Yes, Master Bacon."

Francis nodded slowly, though his chest tightened. "I... understand."

That night, after the clerks had departed and their mother had retreated to her room, Francis wandered alone through the hallways. Every room looked familiar yet strange, like he was seeing them through water.

His father's absence haunted every corner. Eventually, Francis escaped to the garden. The winter wind nipped at his face, but he didn't mind. The cold made the world feel sharp, real. He sat beneath the bare branches of the pear tree, pulling his knees up under his cloak.

Limited funds. Younger sons get less. Earn your own way.

He whispered the words aloud, letting them sting. He had always assumed talent was enough, that learning would open doors. But now the doors seemed to be closing all at once. He pressed his hands into the frozen ground.

"What am I supposed to do now?" he asked the universe.

For a moment, only the wind answered. Then footsteps approached softly across the frost.

Anthony sat beside him. "I thought I'd find you out here."

Francis didn't look up. "Everything changed so fast."

Anthony exhaled. "It always does."

Francis clenched the grass. "I know I should be thinking clearly. Reasoning. But I... I just feel scared."

Anthony put an arm around his shoulders. "You're allowed to feel scared, Francis. You're not made of stone."

Francis's voice shook. "I thought Father would guide me. Now I must do everything alone."

Anthony squeezed him gently. "Not alone. You have me. And Mother. And your mind."

Francis closed his eyes. "But is that enough?"

Anthony didn't answer immediately. Then he said softly, "It will have to be."

In the following days, Francis learned more about the world than he ever had in books.

He learned that in 16th-century England, money flowed like a river, but not everyone drank from it equally. Inheritance laws favored firstborn sons. Younger sons had to carve their way through scholarship, the church, or the mercy of wealthy patrons.

He learned that status could open doors, but could also slam them shut.

He learned that education was expensive. Living was expensive. And people with limited funds had... limited options.

Lady Bacon explained it as gently as she could. "We will support your studies as best we can," she assured him. "But you must be strategic. Wise. Opportunities will be fewer than before."

Francis nodded, trying to look steady. Inside, fear and determination wrestled each other. He promised himself he would not break.

He would rethink everything — his plans, his goals, his path. He would shape his future the way he shaped his experiments: with careful steps and clear thought. But even then, when he told himself all of this, he still felt a flicker of anger. Not at his father. Not at the law. At the unfairness of it all.

If talent mattered... why did wealth matter more? Francis returned to his notebook — slower this time, heavier.

He wrote: *Cause: Father's death. Effect: loss of income, loss of position, loss of certainty.*

Cause: Inheritance laws. Effect: Anthony and I must find our own place through merit.

Cause: Change. Effect: I must change too.

He paused. Then he wrote something new: *If the world will not open to me easily, I will have to open it myself.*

He stared at the sentence until it stopped trembling. A week later, Francis walked through the garden again, pulling his cloak tighter around himself. He stood beside the pear tree and looked up at the sky. Spring would come. Not now. Not soon. But eventually. And the world, though cold, felt full of possibilities: hidden, complicated, demanding possibilities.

Anthony approached, hands tucked beneath his cloak. "You look less miserable," he said.

Francis cracked a tiny smile. "A little."

Anthony stepped beside him. "You know... some people grow best after everything around them changes."

Francis nodded slowly. "Perhaps I am one of those people."

"You are," Anthony said firmly. "You always have been."

Francis exhaled. The sadness didn't disappear, not yet, but it shifted, making room for something sturdier. Resolve. Things would be harder now. He could not rely on comfort. He could not drift on family success. He could not wait for the world to choose him. He would have to choose the world for himself.

That night before bed, Francis opened his notebook again. His father had once praised him for keeping it. "A sharp mind leaves a trail of thoughts," Sir Nicholas had said. Francis let his finger trace the edge of the page.

Then he wrote: *Father is gone. But his belief in me remains. I must build something worthy of it.*

He closed the notebook slowly. For the first time since his father's death, he felt not only grief, but direction.

The house felt quieter now, the halls dimmer, the rooms more spacious in their emptiness. But Francis Bacon, small and thoughtful and determined, was changing inside those same halls. He would not forget this moment. He would not forget what had been taken. And he would not forget that the world was suddenly different.

Because now he knew something he hadn't understood before: talent mattered. Ambition mattered. But without opportunity, neither attribute could grow.

If opportunity would not come to him, he would learn to create it. And that decision — the quiet one made in the cold of grief — would shape everything that came after.

V

4

EXPERIMENTS IN SECRET

Francis Bacon had something more powerful than noble titles or glittering court gossip. He was curious. Not the light, fluttery kind that helped you pass a boring lesson, but the deep, gravitational kind that pulled you toward a question so strongly you could think of nothing else. And so, Francis, now old enough to wander Gray's Inn without constant supervision, began conducting experiments.

Quietly. Secretly. In borrowed corners of halls, gardens, and storage rooms. Not because he wanted to hide, but because people stared.

Whenever they found him bending over a strange setup — water bowls, herbs, scraps of metal — he always heard the same whispered phrase: "Odd young man."

Francis didn't mind. Odd was simply another way of saying "interested."

The first secret laboratory wasn't really a laboratory at all. It was the corner of a chilly storage building behind the gardens.

The gardener, Old Merrit, didn't mind Francis poking around. He just asked that Francis not "explode anything, scorch anything, or summon demons," which Francis promised he had no plans to do.

Still, Merrit would pause now and then as Francis carried in various bowls and jars.

"Another test, Master Bacon?" Merrit would grumble.

"Yes," Francis replied cheerfully.

"What's this one for?"

"I'm testing whether plants grow faster in warm water or cold water."

Merrit blinked. "And you need five identical metal cups for that?"

"Yes," Francis said, "for consistency."

Merrit scratched his beard as if Francis had spoken Greek. Then he shuffled away, muttering, "Odd young man."

Once alone, Francis drew out his small brown notebook. Today's question: *Does warm water help seeds sprout?*

Step 1: Observe - In the garden, seeds seemed to wake faster in soil warmed by sunlight.

Step 2: Hypothesize - Maybe warmth encourages growth.

Step 3: Test- Three cups with warm water.

Three cups with cold. Each with identical seeds, identical soil, identical placement.

Anthony peeked in halfway through the setup. "You realize you look like you're preparing a miniature banquet for mice," he said.

Francis smiled. "If they attend, they'll have to record data."

Anthony shook his head. "You're the strangest brother in England."

But there was no malice in his voice, only pride and amusement.

For days, Francis visited the cups at dawn, midday, and dusk, checking heights, moisture, and any sign of green. He recorded everything — every measurement, every note.

On the fourth morning, a tiny sprout appeared in one of the

warm-water cups. He bent low, his breath fogging in the cold air, and whispered, "Hello there."

He felt triumphant, not because he had confirmed his hypothesis, but because the world had finally answered back. Knowledge, he realized, was like planting seeds. You buried a question in the soil, watered it with effort, and waited for truth to push its way into the light. Sometimes slowly. Sometimes unexpectedly. But always honestly.

And once the first sprout appeared, other experiments followed, each more ambitious than the last.

The Freezing Water Experiment

It began when Francis noticed frost forming on the garden gate one morning.

He wondered: *Does water always freeze at the same speed? Or does it depend on where you place it?*

He brought out jars filled to equal levels with water. He placed one under a stone ledge, one on an exposed table, and one in a shallow ditch. Anthony found him crouched in the frost taking notes.

"Most people enjoy winter from indoors," Anthony observed, teeth chattering.

"You're welcome to go inside," Francis said without looking up. "But freezing is critical to data collection."

Francis tracked the time until ice formed on each jar and scribbled observations furiously.

Hypothesis? *Colder air = faster freezing.*

Result? "Correct," he murmured, watching ice glitter like glass in the morning sun.

The Heating Experiment–Another day he borrowed Merrit's metal ladle to test whether different materials heated at different speeds.

He warmed wax, sand, and water over identical flames (very small flames—Merrit's rules still applied).

His conclusion? *Different substances responded differently to heat.*

This thrilled him. It meant the world wasn't random. It had patterns.

Francis was beginning to see how much of nature followed laws, even if people had not named them yet.

Francis soon created a ritual for every experiment, and he wrote it repeatedly in his notebook:

1. Ask a clear question. What will freeze fastest? What heats fastest? What makes plants grow strong?

2. Predict the answer. "This will occur because…"

3. Test it carefully. Same size jars, same amount of liquid. Same size flames. Same type of soil.

4. Watch closely with all senses. Smell the wax. Hear the crack of frost. See the smallest change.

5. Record the results exactly. No guessing. No exaggeration.

6. Compare the results with your prediction. If you were wrong, wonder why.

7. Ask a new question. Always forward. Always deeper.

He liked this rhythm — steady, patient, and dependable. The world no longer felt like a fog of hearsay and old books. It felt like a puzzle whose pieces he could actually place.

England, like much of Europe, was changing. Some scholars clung tightly to ancient texts, repeating the same ideas simply because old voices had said them first. Others: artists, explorers, thinkers — were beginning to question. Observe. Experiment. This shift — the Renaissance shift — was subtle but powerful.

Francis felt himself pulled into it like a tide. But when he tried to explain his experiments to older scholars, they gave him the same frustrated sigh: "Master Bacon, truth is discovered through reading, not tinkering."

Francis nodded politely. Then he tinkered anyway. He

wasn't trying to be rebellious. He simply believed there must be a more reliable way to understand the world. Books held wisdom. Yes. But nature held evidence.

One afternoon, Francis was balancing two bowls of water in the courtyard, trying to compare evaporation rates.

A passing instructor paused and frowned. "Master Bacon," he said, "why are you staring at bowls?"

"Because water disappears," Francis answered.

"Yes, that is evaporation," the man said impatiently.

"But why?" Francis pressed. "And how fast? And does moving air matter? And what..."

The instructor waved him off. "All these answers exist in Aristotle. Read him."

"I have," Francis said.

"And?"

"And I have questions Aristotle didn't."

That earned him a confused glare.

Another instructor found him heating sand in pots and muttered, "Odd young man." A servant noticed Francis timing shadows with a stick and whispered, "Strange." A laundress spotted him pacing with a jar of river water and told Merrit, "Your scholar's lost his wits."

Merrit grunted. "Suppose it's better than losing his manners."

But Francis didn't mind any of it, because something more important than approval was happening: His notebook was filling with truth.

Francis sat under a crooked pear tree one afternoon, flipping through the pages. He saw scribbled diagrams, lists of materials, times, measurements, smudges of dirt and wax. But to him, the messy pages glowed. This wasn't just a notebook anymore. It was a map. A growing record of how to understand the world, not by trusting old voices but by looking with his own eyes.

Anthony dropped onto the grass beside him. "Still experimenting?"

Francis nodded.

Anthony plucked a hanging pear. "And what have you discovered today?"

Francis grinned. "That plants thrive in warmth. Water freezes faster when exposed to the open air. Wax melts faster than sand. And that most people don't appreciate curiosity."

Anthony laughed. "Well, at least one person does."

Francis raised an eyebrow. "Who?"

"Me," Anthony said.

Francis nudged him lightly. "You're family; it's required."

"Even still," Anthony countered.

They sat quietly for a moment, the afternoon sun warming their backs.

Then Anthony said, "What do you hope all this will lead to? These experiments. These notes."

Francis looked down at his notebook.

"To truth," he said softly. "Not the kind people argue about. The kind that exists whether we like it or not."

Anthony nodded slowly. "And you think your little seeds of knowledge will grow into something big?"

Francis smiled. "Every tree begins with a seed."

That night, Francis gathered his scattered tools, jars, candles, pebbles, scraps of parchment, and stored them neatly in the corner of his makeshift lab. He looked around the dim room. It wasn't much. But it was his. A quiet place where questions could grow.

He placed his notebook on the table like a cherished treasure.

He whispered, "Tomorrow I'll learn something new."

Because knowledge, he knew now, behaved like seeds: plant them carefully, water them with patience, and eventually, even in secret, they would break the soil and rise toward the light.

Francis blew out the candle.

Darkness filled the room, but inside him, the world was brightening, one experiment at a time.

5

FRIEND... WITH A
DANGEROUS FUTURE

Francis Bacon was not supposed to be thinking about the truth that afternoon. He was supposed to be sitting politely in his mother's drawing room while the servants prepared for the arrival of an important guest. His mother paced the floorboards in swift, decisive steps, adjusting cushions, straightening candlesticks, and occasionally inspecting Francis's collar with the intensity of someone checking for structural damage.

"Stand up straight," she said, though he already was.

"Mother, I'm not a child."

"Do not fidget."

Francis realized she was speaking to herself as much as she was to him.

"And for heaven's sake, when he arrives, speak clearly."

Francis pushed his notebook under his chair with the side of his foot. "Yes, Mother."

Anthony lounged near the fireplace, biting back a smile. When their mother left to fetch something, Anthony leaned toward Francis. "Who is this lord again?"

Francis shrugged. "Mother said his name is Robert Devereux, the Earl of Essex."

Anthony's eyebrows rose. "The Queen's favorite?"

"So I've been told."

Anthony whistled. "Then brace yourself. Her favorites are never... quiet."

Francis doubted anything could be louder than his mother's frantic straightening until the front doors flew open with the force of a small hurricane.

A voice boomed down the hall: "Lady Bacon! Forgive my late arrival. My horse and I had a disagreement about speed, and naturally, I won."

Anthony murmured, "Here we go."

Then Essex entered. He was four years younger than Francis, but his confidence and demeanor made him appear older.

He filled the doorway instantly — tall, bright-eyed, every gesture bold. He carried himself with the unshakable certainty of someone accustomed to admiration. His boots were dusted with road dirt that he did not bother brushing off. His smile was as wide as summer and twice as blinding.

"Lady Bacon!" he exclaimed again. "These must be your sons."

He strode forward, taking Anthony's hand in a firm handshake before turning his attention to Francis.

"You must be Francis Bacon."

"I am," Francis said, trying not to sound startled.

Essex took his hand with surprising gentleness, but still with that overwhelming presence behind it. "I have heard remarkable things. They say you read more than a scholar twice your age."

"Only some scholars," Francis replied cautiously.

Essex laughed loudly. "Humility! Excellent, though I can't relate to it."

Francis blinked, unsure how to respond. Anthony coughed into his sleeve to hide a grin.

Essex threw himself into a chair with the easy grace of someone who had never been told "no" in his life. "Now, tell me," he said, leaning forward eagerly, "what grand questions are occupying that brilliant mind of yours today?"

Francis hesitated. Most people, when they asked him what he was thinking about, regretted it immediately.

But Essex looked genuinely interested, his eyes bright with curiosity, not boredom.

So Francis said, "I have been wondering how people make decisions. Some choose through logic, and others through emotion."

Essex slapped the arm of his chair. "Splendid! And which do you prefer?"

"Logic," Francis said. "It allows for careful reasoning."

"And I," Essex declared, tapping his chest proudly, "am ruled entirely by passion."

Anthony muttered, "We can tell."

Essex beamed at him. "You say that as if it's a flaw."

Francis folded his hands neatly. "Not a flaw. But passion can lead to impulsiveness."

Essex threw back his head in laughter. "Impulsiveness is simply courage without waiting."

"Or caution without thinking," Anthony said.

Essex waved him off with a dramatic flourish. "Small details!"

Francis watched Essex closely. The young nobleman radiated confidence — pure, unfiltered, blazing confidence. It was dazzling. It was also unsettling. There was a spark in Essex that felt... unpredictable. Like a lit torch near dry straw. Impressive. Charming. And dangerous if tipped the wrong way.

Over the next hour, Essex spoke freely of court: Queen Elizabeth's sharp wit, political arguments, hunts, dances, duels, victories. He never told stories quietly. Even his sighs were dramatic.

Francis listened with interest, occasionally asking questions that made Essex's face light up.

"You think differently," Essex said finally, studying him with warm intensity. "You don't speak to impress. You speak to understand."

"I try," Francis said.

Essex sat back, eyes narrowing with pleased calculation. "I want to help you."

Anthony tensed. "Help him how?"

"As his patron!" Essex spread his hands as though presenting a treasure chest. "I shall introduce him at court. Speak of his brilliance. Ensure he rises."

Francis blinked. Patronage was how many people advanced in Tudor England, through the support of someone powerful. But being guided by someone as bold and unpredictable as Essex felt a little like being offered a ride on a spirited horse: exciting, flattering... and possibly dangerous.

Francis chose his words carefully. "I am honored. But surely you have many other duties..."

"Nonsense!" Essex said. "A mind like yours must be elevated. I shall bring your name straight to the Queen."

Anthony leaned in and whispered, "Stop him."

Francis stood quickly. "Perhaps we should discuss this later."

"Later?" Essex said indignantly. "Later is for cautious men and cowards! I will go now!"

He practically bounded toward the door.

Francis hurried after him. "My Lord, wait..."

But Essex was already outside, mounting his horse with a flourish that made the stable boy gape.

Francis reached him just as Essex grabbed the reins.

"Lord Devereux, I appreciate your confidence, truly. But the Queen values order, not..." Francis searched for the word.

"Dramatic surprises," Anthony supplied behind him.

Essex grinned. "Then she will appreciate my introducing her to a brilliant mind."

Francis winced. "I just... think caution might..."

But Essex was already galloping away.

"Be wise," Francis finished weakly.

Anthony placed a sympathetic hand on his shoulder. "You do realize he is going to drag you into trouble someday?"

Francis sighed. "Maybe."

"And you're going to let him?"

Francis looked down at his fingers. "If he heeds my counsel, maybe I can keep him from riding off a cliff."

Anthony groaned. "Francis, that boy doesn't avoid cliffs; he runs toward them."

Later that evening, Francis wandered into the quiet garden behind the house, letting the cool night air settle his thoughts. He sat under the old pear tree, his favorite spot, and pulled out his notebook.

He wrote: *Logic can slow the mind but sharpen judgment. Emotion can quicken the heart but cloud reason. Some people are carried by thought; others, by passion.*

He paused and added: *And some, like Essex, are carried by the wind.*

As he wrote, a gust of wind rustled the branches overhead. A pear dropped onto the grass beside him with a heavy thud. Francis flinched.

Anthony's voice floated from behind the tree. "Is that a sign?"

Francis smiled faintly. "If it is, I'm not sure what it means."

Anthony sat beside him. "I know what it means: Essex is going to explode into your life like a dropped fruit."

Francis gently turned the pear over in his hands. "Perhaps. But storms can bring rain, which the earth needs."

"And they can snap branches," Anthony countered.

Francis didn't disagree.

But he also couldn't deny the excitement Essex inspired. The idea of someone powerful believing in him, speaking for him, lifting him, felt like sunlight. Dangerous sunlight perhaps, but sunlight nonetheless.

Two days later, Essex returned.

Bursting through the gate. Laughing. Radiant. Triumphant.

"Francis!" he shouted before Francis had even reached the courtyard. "The Queen listened to me!"

Francis felt his heartbeat stutter.

"She wants to hear more about you," Essex continued. "She loves cleverness. She says England thrives when bright minds speak boldly, and I said you were the brightest I knew!"

Anthony muttered, "Wonderful. The Queen now expects Francis to be bold."

Essex clapped Francis on the back hard enough to make him stagger. "You and I, Francis, we are going to shake the foundations of England!"

Shake the foundations.

The words rang in Francis's mind like a bell.

Part of him thrilled to hear it.

Another part, quieter but sharper, whispered a warning: Foundations do not enjoy being shaken. And Essex, brilliant, vibrant Essex, doesn't shake gently.

Francis managed a small, steady smile. "Then I suppose we must be careful."

Essex laughed. "Careful? Where's the glory in that?"

Francis felt tightness in his chest, not fear exactly, something more complicated. Admiration. Concern. And above all, a sense of something beginning. Something large. Something that would change everything.

That night, Francis returned to the pear tree and opened his notebook.

On a fresh page, he wrote: *Today, a door opened.*

He hesitated... and then added: *And though I cannot yet see what lies beyond it, I know this: Essex is both opportunity and risk. A friend... with a dangerous future.*

He closed the notebook, feeling the cool night breeze brush across his face. Above him, the branches swayed. The air shifted. A storm was forming somewhere beyond the horizon. And Francis, quiet, thoughtful, logical Francis, would one day be standing in the very center of it.

6

A REBELLION OF IDEAS...
AND ONE REAL ONE

Francis Bacon knew trouble before he saw it.

Trouble, in his experience, always announced itself first as a whisper. And lately, London whispered one name everywhere: *Essex.*

Not the brilliant, charming Essex Francis had once admired. Not the generous, ambitious patron who burst into rooms like sunlight. But Essex, the frustrated general. Essex, the insulted favorite. Essex, the man who felt the Queen slipping away from him and was panicking.

Francis could feel something tightening in the air, like the charged stillness before something went terribly wrong. And on a cold February morning, it arrived. The knock on Francis's door startled him out of his notes. He had been writing about natural observations, his latest obsession, and nearly spilled ink across the page.

"Enter," he called, wiping his fingers.

The door swung open. Essex stood there. Boots splattered with mud. Eyes urgent. Posture stiff with determination.

"Francis," he said, breathless, "I need your counsel."

Francis's stomach dropped. "Robert," he said softly, "you look... troubled."

Anthony edged in from the adjoining room, eyebrows raised in silent alarm.

Troubled was an understatement. Essex looked like a man wearing armor beneath his clothes — heavy, strained, ready for war.

Essex shut the door behind him. "The Queen refuses to listen. She humiliates me. Strips me of favor. Treats me like an errand boy."

Francis swallowed. "She restrains you because your judgment has grown..."

"Don't say rash," Essex snapped.

Francis didn't. But the word hung between them anyway.

Essex began pacing. "I went to Ireland at the Queen's command. I tried to do what she wanted, but it was impossible. And now she blames me for failing!"

Francis exchanged a glance with Anthony. The Irish campaign had been a disaster, supplies mismanaged, alliances misread, Essex acting with far too much independence. He had even abandoned the field to rush back to England against orders.

But Francis also knew Essex's pride had always been larger than his caution.

"Robert," he said carefully, "the Queen has given you chance after chance."

Essex shook his head. "She used me. Then cast me aside."

Francis rose slowly. "What are you planning?"

Essex stopped pacing. His voice dropped. "A march."

Anthony inhaled sharply. "A... march?"

"Through London," Essex said. "The citizens adore me. They'll rise. We'll remove the Queen's corrupt advisors. The people will demand justice!"

Francis felt his pulse quicken. This wasn't a whisper

anymore. This was a misfortune; this was shouting and could only end in disaster.

"Robert," Francis said firmly, "this is treason. There must be another way."

Essex met his eyes. "This is righteousness, and it must be done."

"No," Francis replied. "This is dangerous. For you, and for England."

Essex clenched his fists. "I thought you'd understand, thought you were my friend. Isn't this what you talk about? Challenging old ideas? Change? Rebellion against stale thinking?"

Francis shook his head. "Ideas, yes. Rebellion against the Queen? Never, it can't be."

Francis had always believed in careful change, ideas refined through thought, debate, truth. Essex believed in spectacle and adoration.

"Listen to me," Francis urged. "You are fighting the wrong enemy. The Queen isn't the obstacle; you are. Your pride. Your temper. Your desire to be adored is clouding your judgment."

Essex's face tightened, wounded.

Francis stepped closer. "If you march, the Queen will crush you. The court will abandon you. And I..." He hesitated.

Essex leaned in. "You what?"

Francis's voice cracked. "I won't be able to defend you."

Anthony looked down. Essex looked betrayed.

A long silence filled the room.

Then Essex turned away. "I thought you would support me; the way I supported you when you were in need."

"I am supporting you," Francis whispered, "which is why I'm begging you to stop before you cross the line, and this becomes something no one can stop."

But Essex was no longer listening.

"I march at dawn," he said. And he left.

The door closed behind him with a soft click, but to Francis, it sounded like a slam.

The rebellion, when it came, was quick and chaotic. Essex and about two hundred followers marched through the streets of London, shouting for support, calling citizens to rise against the "corrupt council that misled the Queen."

What Essex didn't understand was that Londoners were tired of drama. They wanted bread, safety, and peace, not another noble's temper tantrum. People watched from windows. Some whispered. But no one joined him. The rebellion fizzled in less than a day. By evening, Essex was surrounded at his own house. His followers scattered. He surrendered. And London exhaled in relief.

Francis watched from a distance as soldiers marched Essex away in chains. Anthony stood beside him, jaw tight.

"He thought the people would follow him," Anthony said.

Francis nodded. "He mistook admiration for support."

Anthony added quietly, "He mistook pride for strength."

Francis closed his eyes. Essex had wanted glory. But the irony, sharp and painful, was this: He found disaster instead.

The next morning, messengers arrived at Gray's Inn. Francis was summoned to Her Majesty's Most Honorable Privy Council. He knew what that meant. Anthony walked with him through the courtyard. The winter sun cast long shadows across the cobblestones — cold, stretched, uncertain.

"You don't have to speak against him," Anthony said quietly.

Francis shook his head. "I know, but I do have to tell the truth. I serve the Crown, and value the truth wherever the evidence leads."

"And Robert?"

Francis's voice turned small. "I serve him too. In my own way."

Anthony frowned. "How is betraying him serving him?"

Francis stopped walking. "By telling the truth. Someone must. Lies won't save him, can't save him."

Anthony opened his mouth but closed it again. He understood. But he hated it. Francis faced forward again. Reason told him that what Essex had done was wrong. Evidence showed the rebellion clearly. The Crown would demand justice. England demanded stability. But emotion? Emotion twisted inside him like a blade; why didn't he listen to reason?

Science taught Francis to separate fact from feeling. Politics demanded it. Duty required it. But friendship? Friendship complicated everything. He whispered to himself, "*Truth first. Even when it hurts.*"

When Francis entered the council chamber, Queen Elizabeth sat at the head of the long table, her presence as sharp and commanding as ever. She was older now, but age had only hardened her authority.

Her eyes lifted to Francis as he bowed.

"Master Bacon," she said, "your friend has endangered my kingdom."

"Yes, Your Majesty," Francis said softly.

"You have known him since we were young," she continued. "Tell us, why has he done this?"

Francis felt all eyes turn toward him. Judges.

Advisors. Witnesses. He forced himself to breathe.

"Because he believed," Francis said slowly, "that he deserved more than the role he was given. He believed the people adored him, that the court misunderstood him. He let pride blind him to what was required of him."

Elizabeth's gaze sharpened. "And what do you believe?"

Francis swallowed. "I believe he was misguided. But I also believe he loved England. Deeply."

A murmur rolled through the room.

Elizabeth studied him. "And what must be done with such a man?"

Francis's voice nearly failed. But he managed to say: "Your Majesty... whatever you decide must be for the stability of the realm. Not for personal vengeance. Not for fear. For England."

Elizabeth nodded, her expression unreadable. "Spoken like a true servant of the Crown."

Francis bowed again, his heart heavy. He knew what was coming. That night, back in his room, Francis sat at his desk with his small brown notebook open before him. The same notebook where he had once written observations about birds, stars, and experiments.

Now he wrote something else: *Reason can separate truth from feeling. But it cannot erase pain.*

I warned him. I tried. But a man running toward disaster does not pause for advice.

He paused, then added: *I must hold both truths: I cared for him. And I could not follow him.*

The ink shimmered in the candlelight.

Anthony appeared in the doorway, leaning heavily against the frame. "Francis," he said softly, "did you do the right thing?"

Francis kept his eyes on the page. "I did what England needed."

Anthony exhaled. "That's not what I asked."

Francis closed the notebook, pressing his hand against the cover as if holding something fragile inside.

"No," he whispered. "But it's the only answer I can live with."

The rebellion had been small, short, doomed from the start. But for Francis Bacon, its consequences were enormous. It forced him to choose. It forced him to think beyond loyalty, beyond friendship, beyond fear. It forced him to witness up close what happened when emotion overpowered reason. A lesson he would never forget.

And a lesson that would shape the method he would one day give to the world: Truth must be tested, even when it hurts. Especially when it hurt.

Francis set the notebook aside and extinguished the candle. The room darkened, but inside him, a single thought remained: *"It's not what we profess, but what we practice that gives us integrity."*

The rebellion was over. But the revolution inside him had begun.

7

THE TRIAL OF A FRIEND

Francis Bacon had always believed that truth could be examined and tested like a mineral or a flame, but nothing in the world had prepared him for the kind of truth he now faced.

Not a scientific truth. Not a philosophical truth. But the hard truth that sometimes hurts.

The truth that his friend, his former patron, Robert Devereux, Earl of Essex, had committed treason.

Francis sat alone in his chamber at Gray's Inn, hands folded before him, listening to the fire crackle weakly. The sound reminded him of thin ice fracturing. A small, dangerous sound that carried the threat of a larger break.

A parchment lay before him, sealed with the Privy Council's mark. A summons. He had to testify.

Anthony stood by the window, staring out at the gray evening. "You don't have to read it again," he said quietly. "We know what it says."

Francis closed his eyes. "I need to understand it."

"You already do," Anthony replied.

Francis pressed his fingertips into his temples. "Understanding... and accepting... are different."

Anthony approached slowly. His footsteps were soft, matching the heaviness of the room. "This is not your fault. Essex made his choices."

Francis didn't answer, because deep down, in the place he kept locked behind logic and discipline, he wasn't entirely sure that was true.

Earlier that morning, two royal messengers had delivered the summons. Their expressions had been stiff, their uniforms immaculate, as if the severity of their task demanded perfection even in posture.

Francis had broken the seal with shaking hands. The words struck him like blows. *You are commanded to appear before the court to give testimony regarding the Earl of Essex.*

Anthony had read over his shoulder and exhaled sharply. "It's official then. They will make an example of him."

Francis felt the air around him thin.

Essex, brilliant Essex, reckless Essex, had once treated Francis like a younger brother. He had helped him, encouraged him, and introduced him to powerful allies. He had also expected loyalty in return. Dangerous loyalty.

And now, Francis would speak at a trial that could end in his execution.

Anthony said nothing more. He simply sat beside Francis and waited for the first shock to pass. But it didn't. It only grew heavier.

Two days later, Francis walked through the stone corridors leading to the trial chamber. His steps echoed. He felt as though the sound might fracture something within him.

Elizabethan trials were not like the fair, measured proceedings he dreamed England might have someday. They were swift. Evidence was read. Testimony delivered. The crown's interest often overshadowed nuance. The monarchy ruled.

The law followed.

Francis's breath caught as he approached the doors. He could already hear voices inside, murmurs thick with accusation.

Anthony walked with him until the doorway. "I'll wait outside."

"Thank you," Francis whispered.

He stepped into the chamber. The air tasted of tension, dry, metallic, expectant. Essex stood in the center, guarded on all sides. His once-proud posture had wilted slightly, as if the weight of his choices had finally settled. He looked older. Tired. Haunted. Their eyes met. A flash of something passed between them. Recognition. Regret. Maybe betrayal.

Francis's throat tightened. He wanted to look away but couldn't. Not yet. Not when this might be the last time he saw the man alive.

The clerk called out, "Master Francis Bacon, Counselor to the Crown."

A ripple moved through the chamber. Everyone knew Francis had once served Essex. Everyone also knew he now served the Queen.

He stepped forward slowly, as if the floor were uneven beneath him. Documents were placed before him. Letters. Reports. Statements from witnesses. Diagrams showing the routes Essex's men had taken during their attempted uprising. These were facts. Hard, undeniable facts.

Francis stared down at them, remembering Essex not as a traitor but as the charming, impulsive young man who once invited him to ride through Hyde Park at dawn.

"How do you separate friendship from duty?" a voice inside him whispered.

He answered silently, *"With the same method I apply to science. Look at the evidence. Not the emotion."*

But this evidence cut deeper than any experiment he had ever conducted.

A judge spoke. "Sir Francis Bacon, do you recognize these letters?"

Francis forced his voice to remain steady. "I do."

"Did the Earl of Essex seek to raise support against the Crown?"

Francis hesitated. Essex stared at him from across the chamber.

Francis swallowed. "Yes."

"Did he, in your judgment, willfully endanger the stability of England?"

Francis closed his eyes for a single heartbeat. In them, he saw flashes of memory: Essex laughing under a summer tree. Essex training for war. Essex whispering schemes he never should have spoken. Essex warning Francis to be bold—too bold.

When he opened his eyes again, he answered: "Yes."

The word fell heavy into the silence, like a stone dropping into deep water. Essex flinched, barely, but enough for Francis to see.

A murmur spread through the chamber. Some officials nodded. Others watched Francis with unreadable expressions. Francis stood stiffly, feeling guilt twist through him like a cold wind.

When the questioning paused, Francis was dismissed until later in the day. He left the chamber and leaned against the stone wall, trying to catch his breath.

Anthony approached. "You told the truth," he said gently.

"But it feels like betrayal," Francis whispered.

Anthony didn't argue. He simply placed a hand on Francis's arm.

Francis pulled out his small brown notebook, the same notebook he'd used since boyhood. The same one filled with questions, observations, contradictions, and seeds of ideas. And now, it held something else. Pain.

He opened to a fresh page and wrote: *Truth can wound. And sometimes the deepest cuts come from honesty.*

He paused, then added: *I must learn to carry truth even when it hurts to hold it.*

As he wrote, the words wavered. His hand trembled slightly. But he finished the line.

Anthony watched him quietly. "Your notebook used to hold curiosities," he said. "Now it holds reality."

Francis nodded. "Both are necessary."

He closed it gently, as if afraid it might break.

When Francis returned to the chamber, Essex was giving his own defense — passionate, eloquent, desperate. He claimed misunderstandings. Miscommunications. Misinterpretations.

His voice cracked once. Only once, but Francis heard it. The judges conferred.

Francis forced himself to analyze the proceedings like a scientist examining a flame: Observation - Essex's actions threatened the crown.

Evidence - letters, testimonies, armed movement.

Variables - Intent, pride, political pressure.

Conclusion - The danger was real.

Emotion clouded the picture, but the facts remained fixed. Critical thinking had never felt so cold. Late afternoon sunlight slanted through the high windows when the verdict was delivered. Guilty.

The word echoed through the chamber, bouncing off stone and settling like dust.

Essex closed his eyes. For a moment, he looked small, just a man, not a leader, not a noble, not a legend in the making. Just human.

Francis felt something inside him fracture.

As the guards moved Essex away, he glanced at Francis one

last time. There was no hatred in his expression, only sorrow. And something like understanding. Francis bowed his head.

Outside, the evening sky had darkened into a charcoal gloom; it seemed fitting. Anthony waited on the steps, worry lining his face.

"Francis," he said softly. "Is it done?"

Francis nodded.

Anthony walked with him in silence as they left the building. Carriages rattled past. Lanterns flickered. London breathed its usual noise, indifferent to the tragedy of a single man.

At last Anthony said, "You did what the Crown demanded. You did what the truth demanded."

Francis's voice was barely a whisper. "Two masters. I served both. And lost one."

Anthony didn't try to comfort him with easy platitudes. He simply walked beside him through the cold.

As they approached Gray's Inn, Francis withdrew his notebook again. He flipped to the fresh entry and read the painful words he had written.

Then, beneath them, he added: *Truth without love becomes cruelty. Love without truth becomes blindness. I must find a way to hold both.*

He closed the notebook slowly.

"Come," Anthony said. "You need rest."

"No," Francis replied. "I need purpose."

Anthony gave a small nod. "Then let this be the weight that strengthens you, not the one that crushes you."

Francis looked up at the night sky. Stars flickered faintly through the clouds — distant, distant truths.

"I will learn from this," he said. "Even if it hurts."

Later, alone in his room, Francis set his notebook on his table and stared at it. For years, that notebook had been a symbol of discovery, a place for wonder, questions, and the beginnings of the ideas that might reshape the world. Tonight, it held pain.

But pain, he realized, was also truth. And truth, no matter how heavy, was something he had vowed to serve.

He touched the book gently. "Let this," he whispered, "shape me toward wisdom."

Then he blew out the candle. Darkness filled the room, but inside Francis's mind, the first sparks of a future method flickered, small but certain. Not all knowledge came with joy. Some came at a sacrifice. And in that sacrifice, something new was being born.

8

ENDINGS AND BEGINNINGS

The house was too still.

Not the stillness of night or sleep, but the kind that settles after a rain washes everything it touches. Francis stood in the doorway of Anthony's chamber, his hand resting against the wood as if the whole structure might collapse if he stopped holding it upright.

Anthony lay propped against a mound of pillows, breath thin as paper. The winter afternoon cast long stripes of pale light across his face, making him look almost transparent. He had grown smaller, so how could a mind so large fit inside something so fragile?

A physician hovered uselessly nearby. "His strength fails by the hour, Sir Francis."

Francis nodded, though the words did not feel real. Everything since the Essex trial had carried that same unreal quality — whispers behind doors, the Queen's unreadable expression, the echo of his own voice condemning the man who once called him brother. The world had tilted then.

Now it felt as if it were falling.

He dismissed the physician with a quiet gesture and moved

to Anthony's side. His brother's eyes fluttered open at the sound of the chair scraping.

"Francis," Anthony whispered, the single word stretching him thin.

Francis forced a steady smile. "You should rest."

Anthony breathed out a faint, humorless laugh. "I have been doing little else."

Francis swallowed. "I'm here. Whatever you need."

"You," Anthony murmured, "should be anywhere but here. You have work at court... letters to answer... fires to put out." His voice rasped. "And enemies to out-think."

"I can out-think them later," Francis said. "You come first."

A shadow flickered across Anthony's face — part gratitude, part sadness, perhaps part fear. He closed his eyes again, gathering what little strength lingered.

"Francis," he said after a long moment, "listen to me carefully."

Francis leaned closer.

"You must stop punishing yourself."

Francis stiffened. "Anthony..."

"No," Anthony breathed, his voice sharper than his body should have allowed. "You think I do not know you? I have watched you blame yourself for Essex, for every word spoken in that chamber, for every choice you did not want to make."

Francis's jaw tightened. "Duty is not always kind."

"It shouldn't devour you," Anthony whispered. "You've always believed that truth is above affection, above comfort. But you forget—truth does not keep you warm at night."

Francis looked down. He didn't trust himself to speak.

Anthony's breathing grew ragged, but he pressed on. "When Essex fell, you lost more than a patron. You lost a piece of yourself. But when I go..." His voice shook.

Francis reached for his hand. "Don't."

"When I go," Anthony repeated, "you must not lose the rest."

The words struck Francis harder than any political blow. Anthony was the one person who had always seen him—past the ambition, the curiosity, the clever arguments, down to the boy under the pear tree counting raindrops. Without him... what remained?

Francis whispered, "I don't know how to do this without you."

Anthony managed a faint smile. "You will, because you must. Your mind is meant for more than grief." His fingers tightened weakly around Francis's. "Just... don't let the world turn you into someone I wouldn't recognize."

Francis blinked hard against the blur in his vision.

They sat in silence, the kind that fills the air with meaning rather than emptiness. Outside, a carriage rattled down the street. Somewhere in the distance, bells tolled the hour.

Anthony's breath began to slow.

"Stay," he whispered.

"I'm here," Francis said. "I'm not leaving."

The final minutes passed softly, like the last pages of a well-read book turning themselves. Anthony's hand became lighter in his grasp. His chest rose once, twice, then no more.

Stillness settled, deep, absolute, irreversible.

Francis did not move. Not when the servants knocked. Not when the physician returned. Not even when someone whispered, "He is gone."

He simply sat, Anthony's hand in his, as if by refusing to let go he could keep the world from collapsing around him.

At last, when the candle guttered low, Francis spoke aloud, to the empty room, to the quiet body, to the universe that had taken too much from him in too short a time.

"First Essex," he whispered. "Now, you."

His throat tightened. "How many more pieces must I give before I become whole?"

There was no answer. Only silence.

But deep within that silence, Francis felt something shifting —not healing, not yet, but hardening. A cold resolve settling like frost on glass.

If the world insisted on stripping away his anchors, then he would build something that could not be taken. Something stronger than favor, stronger than politics, stronger even than grief.

Truth.

A new way to know.

He rose slowly, letting Anthony's hand fall to the sheets.

And for the first time in his life, Francis Bacon walked away from his brother's side feeling truly, unbearably alone.

The night clung to Gray's Inn like damp wool. A thin mist drifted through the courtyard, softening the lamps into pale halos. Francis walked slowly beneath them, as though each flame demanded a moment of contemplation.

He had grown accustomed to walking alone.

Anthony had been gone for less than a year, yet Francis felt as though he had lived a decade since. The world had become quieter in his absence, quieter and hollower. The silence after Anthony's death was not peaceful; it echoed. And echoes followed him everywhere.

As he pushed open the heavy door to the library chamber, he found he was not alone. A figure sat near the hearth, warming his hands over the small, stubborn fire.

"Tobie Matthew, my friend, it is good to see you again," Francis said softly.

Tobie rose, bowing slightly, his eyes bright with that restless intelligence he carried like a second soul. "Forgive the intrusion, Francis. Your servants said you were likely to be here."

Francis nodded, shedding his cloak. "You are welcome. I find few seek me out these days."

Tobie studied him for a long moment—too long, perhaps. But Tobie had never been afraid of looking directly at a man, especially a complicated one.

"I came," he said gently, "because I am concerned about you. You don't seem the same as before."

Francis stiffened. "There is no need for concern. I am working."

"Working," Tobie echoed with a faint, sad smile. "You bury yourself in it as if pages can hold a man upright."

Francis turned away, moving toward the long table strewn with papers. "Work is what remains."

"What remains," Tobie said softly, "after grief takes its share."

Francis stopped. His hands rested on the back of a chair, fingers gripping the carved wood. For a long moment he said nothing. The fire crackled behind them, the only sound bridging the distance Francis kept between himself and the world.

At last he exhaled. "Anthony was half my mind," he said, the words pulled from him like threads unraveling. "He shaped my thoughts before I spoke them. He steadied me when I erred. He knew me... completely."

Tobie stepped forward, but carefully, as if approaching a wounded creature.

"I know," he murmured. "I knew what he meant to you."

Francis's jaw tightened. "And now he is gone. Essex is gone. Elizabeth is fading. Every anchor of my life is slipping away."

Tobie stood beside him now, shoulder to shoulder, though not quite touching. "The world changes," he said. "But minds like yours must not be left to solitude. You are too large for it."

Francis let out a hollow laugh. "Large? I feel diminished."

Tobie reached out and gently, respectfully, placed a hand on Francis's arm. "Then let me be plain. You are a man whom I admire more than any other living thinker. Your vision, your method, your desire to remake knowledge itself... It is extraordinary. And you must not walk through this darkness alone."

Francis finally turned to look at him.

In Tobie's eyes, he saw no flattery, no political angle, no hungry ambition, just sincerity, bright and unwavering. It was a gaze Francis had not received since Anthony's final days.

"You honor me," Francis said quietly.

"I speak truly," Tobie replied. "And if you allow, I will walk beside you. As a friend. As a mind equal in curiosity, if not in breadth. As someone who sees your worth, not your wounds."

A warmth stirred in Francis's chest, unexpected and almost painful. "Why?" he asked. "Why me, Tobie?"

Tobie's smile was soft, but full. "Because the world needs what you are building. And because genius, true genius, should never be left without companionship."

Francis studied him again, closer this time. Tobie's presence was steady, vibrant, carrying a kind of energy that pressed against Francis's isolation. Not a replacement for Anthony; nothing could be, but a bridge out of mourning.

"Tobie," he said slowly, "I would be glad of your friendship."

Tobie inclined his head. "Then it is yours."

The fire crackled again, brighter now, as if in response. Francis moved to the table and gestured for Tobie to sit. Together they leaned over the scattered pages, notes on natural philosophy, drafts of The Advancement of Learning, diagrams of Bacon's early method.

Tobie's eyes lit up. "Francis," he whispered, "this is the future."

Francis felt something settle inside him—not joy, not yet, but a beginning. A return. A reason to keep climbing.

He looked at Tobie and said, "Then help me shape it."

"With pleasure," Tobie replied.

And so the two men bent their heads over the papers, the fire warming their backs while the first true companionship since Anthony's death took root, quietly, steadily, like a candle lit in ruins. A small light. But enough.

9

___

NEW KING, NEW CHANCE

Francis Bacon had lived through the reign of a queen who understood survival better than anyone alive. Elizabeth's court had been a world of sharp glances and sharper consequences, where ideas were weighed, measured, and often dismissed before they ever reached daylight. Everything was tight and careful, like a lute string pulled one twist too far, always on the edge of snapping.

But now the lute string had slackened. Elizabeth was gone. James Stuart, King James VI of Scotland, now James I of England, had arrived like a gust of northern wind blowing open locked doors.

Francis stood in the royal hall waiting to greet the new king, adjusting the cuffs of his coat and trying not to pace. Tobie leaned against a pillar behind him, studying the incoming swarm of nobles with thinly masked amusement.

"Does everyone look more hopeful?" Tobie Matthew murmured. "Or is it simply that they are all trying to impress the new king?"

Francis smiled at his friend. "Both probably, but can you feel it?"

Tobie blinked. "Feel what?"

"The looseness," Francis said. "Like the kingdom has finally unclenched its jaw."

Tobie smirked. "Elizabeth would not appreciate that metaphor."

"No," Francis said. "But that is precisely the point."

Before Tobie could reply, a herald trumpeted loudly enough to startle several diplomats into dropping their scrolls.

"His Most Gracious Majesty, King James of England, Scotland, and Ireland!"

The hall shifted, parting like a wave, as the king strode in. Francis's first thought was: *He walks fast.*

James moved with unexpected energy, his robes swishing like restless waves around him. He patted shoulders, barked greetings, laughed too loudly, asked three questions before anyone answered one, and waved off bows if they lasted too long.

Elizabeth had been a cautious moon pulling tides in controlled arcs. James was a comet — bright, unpredictable, and impossible to ignore.

Tobie leaned in. "He looks like he hasn't slept."

"He looks," Francis whispered, "like he reads."

When it was Francis's turn to bow, James stepped forward eagerly.

"Bacon!" James boomed. "I ha'e long been desirous tae mak' yer acquaintance! They tell me ye possess a mind o' such great sharpness that it could peel the very husk frae the kernel o' truth."

Francis bowed lower to hide his startled grin. "Your Majesty is generous."

"Nonsense. I do love clever men." James clapped Francis on both shoulders with enough force to nearly knock him off balance. "England needs mair thinking. Scotland as well— though dinna tell my ain folk I said that."

Francis straightened. "I share Your Majesty's love of learning."

"Yes!" James said, eyes sparkling. "Learning! It's the lifeblood o' a strong kingdom. Though, to be fair, I've aye got a fondness for hunting and a bit o' poetry—but learning most of all."

"Then England is fortunate," Francis said, "for she has long needed a king who values knowledge."

James beamed. "Och, you flatter fine."

"I mean, honestly," Francis said.

Tobie whispered, "Francis, beware. Compliments are flammable around royalty."

James waved Tobie forward. "Ah, the Friend! I've heard o' your letters. The two o' ye must plague London wi' your cleverness."

Tobie bowed. "We try."

James laughed. "Good! Plague it! Heaven kens it needs a guid shaking."

Then the king turned to Francis with sudden, earnest seriousness. "I hear you think the world must seek truth in new ways. Through testing. Observing. No' just reading auld books." Francis's breath caught.

"You have... heard correctly," he said.

James leaned closer. "Tell me mair."

It wasn't a command. It was an invitation.

And in that moment, Francis felt the rising action of his own life, like a wheel finally catching traction after years of spinning.

The weeks that followed felt like a shift in the weather, subtle at first, then unmistakable. News of James's preferences spread quickly: the king welcomed scholars, hosted debates, asked questions, and even held late-night discussions where he grilled philosophers like a hungry man tearing into a roast.

Francis attended one such gathering.

Books stacked like miniature towers lined the king's private study. Charts of stars sprawled across tables. Two astronomers argued in the corner. A mathematician was demonstrating geometric ratios with bread rolls.

James spotted Francis and waved him over. "Come here, man! We're arguin' aboot the nature o' comets. Some puir fools still think they're omens. I say they're naught but flaming stanes passin' through the heavens. Whit think ye?"

Francis hesitated. "I think we need more evidence."

"Aye!" James clapped his hands. "A reasonable answer! I approve o' that!"

Tobie muttered, "Careful. He may adopt you as a pet philosopher."

But Francis wasn't worried. For the first time in his life, being curious did not make him suspicious. It made him valuable.

At Elizabeth's court, curiosity had been a candle, one protected carefully, shielding the flame from cold winds of caution. At James's court, curiosity was encouraged to become a torch.

Francis couldn't help comparing the two monarchs. Elizabeth's court had been like a painting, every gesture calculated, every word polished until it could cut. Diplomats tiptoed around her moods like cats navigating glass. She ruled with sharp intelligence and sharper caution.

Her court smelled of lavender, polished brass, and secrets held tight.

James's court smelled of ink, wine, muddy boots, dogs, and excitement.

Where Elizabeth had required brilliance wrapped in

restraint, James wanted brilliance blazing out loud. His halls were louder, fuller, messier, and far more interesting.

Tables overflowed with maps and instruments. Scholars roamed freely. Poets argued with theologians. Lenses, compasses, globes, and star charts littered side rooms.

One day Francis found a Danish astronomer calibrating a makeshift telescope on a windowsill. Elizabeth would have sent him home for scratching the furniture. James fetched him more glass. The shift was not merely cultural; it was political.

Elizabeth had reigned during threats, plots, and religious tension. Stability meant survival. James sought unity and ideas. Stability meant progress. And progress meant opportunity.

A month after James's coronation, Francis was summoned to Whitehall again. Tobie accompanied him, though he insisted it was only to ensure Francis didn't accidentally invent something dangerous on the way.

They were ushered into a smaller audience chamber. James sat at a desk strewn with scrolls and quills, a plate of fruit half-devoured beside a stack of manuscripts.

He waved them in. "Bacon! I've been readin' some o' your auld essays. Grand stuff—fair delicious. Now tell me, why havenae ye written mair?"

Francis blinked. "Your Majesty... I have ideas, but I did not know if..."

"Write!" James thundered. "Write till your fingers drop aff! England needs thinkers—no' just obedient wee scribes."

Tobie whispered, "He definitely likes you."

James continued, "In fact, I mean to promote ye. England must back its philosophers. D'ye agree?"

Francis bowed deeply. "I am grateful, Your Majesty. I only hope to serve with wisdom."

"Wisdom!" James laughed. "A braw word. Keep usin' it. Ye'll need it once the parliamentarians start barkin'."

Francis dared a smile. "I will handle them, sire."

"Excellent," James said, waving them off. "Now away wi' ye —and teach England to think differently."

They left the chamber stunned.

Outside, Tobie grabbed Francis by the shoulders. "He's going to support you."

Francis exhaled slowly, letting the truth settle. "Yes," he said. "For the first time in my life... a king wants my ideas."

Later that evening, Francis walked the garden path near Gray's Inn with a notebook in his hands. The moon hung low, silvering the frost-dusted hedges. Tobie strolled beside him, wrapped in a cloak.

"You look dazed," Tobie said. "Should I fetch a physician?"

"No," Francis said quietly. "Just thinking."

"About the promotion?"

"About what it means."

He stopped walking, turning his face toward the cold night air. "In the past," he said, "great thinkers changed the world despite their rulers."

Tobie nodded. "Galileo comes to mind."

"But imagine," Francis said, "what could happen if rulers supported discovery instead of fearing it."

His breath clouded in the moonlight. "Imagine a king who funds instruments. Laboratories. Observatories."

Tobie said softly, "Imagine a kingdom where curiosity is not dangerous."

Francis looked out over the dark garden. "Yes," he whispered. "Imagine that."

He knew the truth: powerful ideas needed powerful allies. Even the brightest spark required shelter from the wind.

James was that shelter, a king whose weight and influence could tip the entire world toward progress. If Francis could earn his trust... If his ideas could take root in the heart of the monarchy...

Then England itself could become the seedbed of a revolution in knowledge. Not a political revolution. A scientific one.

In the weeks that followed, Francis found himself invited to council meetings, given small tasks, then larger ones. His voice began to matter. His ideas gained ground.

He met scholars from Scotland, mathematicians from France, and translators from the Low Countries. He discussed telescopes, magnetism, anatomy, weather, and machinery with men who actually cared.

This was rising action in the truest sense, not a dramatic battle or crisis, but the rising of opportunity. Possibility. Energy. Everywhere he turned, doors cracked open.

One evening, Francis stood at his desk, looking down at his notebooks filled with scattered thoughts, sketches of experiments, scraps of half-formed theories.

"Perhaps," he murmured, "the dream can live."

"What dream?" Tobie asked from the doorway.

Francis looked up. "The dream of changing how the world learns."

Tobie smiled slowly. "Then I suppose we should start preparing for the consequences."

That night, Francis lit a single candle in his room and sat before a blank sheet of parchment. The kingdom had changed. The leadership had changed.

And now, perhaps, knowledge itself could change.

He touched the quill to the page and whispered: "A new king... a new chance." And he began to write.

. . .

The hall at Whitehall glittered like a field of stars trapped indoors.

Candles flickered in tall iron sconces, throwing gold light across silk banners, polished armor, and the anxious faces of men waiting to be remade by a single touch of steel. Courtiers murmured behind lace-edged sleeves. Pages darted between them like quick, bright birds. Even the stone floor seemed to hum with anticipation.

Francis Bacon stood among the gathered gentlemen, his hands clasped behind his back, the collar of his best doublet sitting stiffly against his throat. He had dressed carefully, too carefully, perhaps, but he felt awkward in the finery. Like a scholar wearing someone else's honor.

He had waited for many things in life: recognition, position, security, a voice in shaping England's future. But knighthood? That had never been the dream. Yet now, as King James prepared to knight dozens of men in celebration of his new reign, Francis found himself among them.

He tried not to think of Anthony, not here, not now, but the ache of absence hovered at the edge of his mind like a bruise. A trumpet sounded. A hush fell over the hall.

King James entered with a theatrical flourish, robes sweeping behind him, the royal sword gleaming at his side. The new King had an air of restless intelligence, sharp eyes, a heavy stride, a face that shifted between mischief and majesty.

James grinned broadly. "Weel then! Let us begin." His Scots burr rolled through the hall like warm thunder.

One by one, the candidates stepped forward. James moved briskly, touch, word, rise; touch, word, rise, bestowing knighthood as if conducting a musical rhythm only he could hear.

Francis waited as the line shortened. His heart beat steadily, but heavily, as though it carried the weight of unspoken thoughts. Politics had taught him patience; grief had taught him silence. But this moment, this moment felt like the beginning of something larger than either.

"Francis Bacon," the herald called.

Francis stepped forward. His steps echoed on the stone, louder than he expected. He knelt on the cushion placed before the throne, lowering himself with practiced care. The hall felt impossibly vast from this angle, ceilings towering, banners sweeping, dozens of gazes fixed upon him.

King James looked down at him, eyes glinting with a mix of fondness and calculation.

"Ah, Mr. Bacon," the King said, his voice warm. "A man o' letters. A man o' the law. A man o' uncommon sense. England shall make guid use o' ye."

Francis bowed his head. "Your Majesty," he murmured.

James drew the ceremonial sword. The blade caught the candlelight in a sudden flash, cold brilliance slicing through the air. Francis felt a tremor chase along his spine.

The King laid the flat of the sword upon Francis's right shoulder, then his left.

"In the name o' God, and Saint George, and Saint Andrew," James declared, "I dub thee knight."

The sword tapped his shoulder again, lighter this time, almost affectionate.

"Rise, Sir Francis Bacon."

Francis stood. The hall felt different from this height. Not physically, he was the same man he had been a moment ago, but something in the room had shifted. The faces watching him now seemed sharper, more measuring. Knights were expected to wield influence, loyalty, and strength. Some envied him. Some resented him. Some would now whisper his name with new interest, or new suspicion.

James leaned slightly toward him. "I foresee ye'll do grand service," he said. "Your mind runs quicker than most. And England needs quick minds thae days."

Francis bowed. "I will serve faithfully, Majesty."

"See that ye do," James said with a smile that was almost a warning. "Ambition's a bonny thing—if ye keep it bridled."

Francis's breath caught. Did the King see ambition in him? Did he fear it? Or did he welcome it?

He stepped back into the crowd, the murmurs swelling around him like rising water.

"Sir Francis."

"A scholar knight—imagine that."

"Perhaps he'll climb further still."

"Aye, but he must watch his footing…"

Francis felt their voices brushing against him — envy, curiosity, dismissal, admiration. A mixture he had long learned to navigate.

But something unexpected tugged at him then: a longing for Anthony. For the one person who would have understood the complexity of this moment — its honor, its cost, its possibilities. Anthony would have teased him, congratulated him, worried for him, and reminded him to remain himself.

Instead, Francis stood alone.

Tobie Matthew appeared at his side as the crowd shifted. His smile was gentle; his eyes were warm with genuine pride.

"Sir Francis," Tobie said, voice bright. "It suits you."

Francis allowed himself a small smile. "Does it?"

"Yes," Tobie said. "Because you will make it mean something. Not many men who were knighted today can say the same."

Francis looked toward the King, then toward the sword, now sheathed again. "Titles are simple things," he murmured. "It is their weight that matters."

"And you," Tobie said softly, "have shoulders built for weight."

Francis felt something ease inside him—not joy, but steadiness. A quiet resolve.

"Come," Tobie added. "Let us leave this crowd before someone mistakes you for a man who enjoys ceremony."

Francis exhaled a low laugh. "A fate worse than any political setback."

They stepped out of the hall together, into the cool corridor where the air felt clearer, less gilded.

Behind them, the hall continued to roar with celebration.

The corridors outside the great hall were calmer now, the echoes of celebration fading into muffled warmth. Francis walked beside Tobie Matthew, letting the cool air wash away the thick scent of candle wax and ambition that clung to the ceremony.

"Sir Francis Bacon," Tobie teased lightly. "You'll grow used to the sound of it."

"I doubt that," Francis replied. "Titles rarely change a man."

Tobie opened his mouth to respond, but footsteps approached from the far end of the gallery, light, quick, accompanied by the soft rustle of silk.

A woman entered the passage.

She was young, far younger than the noble widows and seasoned courtiers who thrived in James's circle. Her gown was a clear, pale blue, the color of morning just before the sun declares itself. A pair of older ladies trailed behind her, whispering sharply, as if her enthusiasm required constant taming.

She stopped when she saw Francis.

Her eyes widened with open curiosity, unguarded and bright. "You were knighted today," she said before the women behind her could intervene.

Francis blinked, startled by her directness. "Yes," he said softly. "A few moments ago."

One of the older ladies stepped forward, flustered. "Lady Alice, please, proper introductions…"

But the girl only smiled. "Alice Barnham," she said, dipping into a graceful, earnest curtsey. "My father insisted I witness the ceremony. He says England is changing faster than we can learn to speak of it."

Francis inclined his head. "An insightful sentiment."

"Is it true," she asked, "that scholars do not like being honored? I watched you when His Majesty touched the sword to your shoulder. You looked... thoughtful."

Tobie coughed lightly into his hand, amused.

Francis found himself at a rare loss for words. "Thoughtful, perhaps," he admitted. "It is a solemn thing to be called to higher duty."

Alice considered this as though turning a gem in her hand. "Then the honor suits you. Too many men today seemed pleased only with the ceremony."

Behind her, the older ladies exchanged horrified glances.

Francis's lips curved. "You are candid, Lady Alice."

Her cheeks flushed, not embarrassed, but pleased. "My tutors complain of it."

"Your tutors," Tobie whispered to Francis, "are wise."

Francis offered her a gentle, respectful nod. "Your father must be proud."

"He is," she said, though a flicker of shyness crossed her face. "He says England needs minds like yours."

Francis felt the weight of the day settle differently then, not as pressure, but as a quiet acknowledgment from an unexpected source.

"Please give him my regards," he said.

"I will." She hesitated, then added softly, "And... congratulations, Sir Francis."

She and her attendants moved down the corridor, their footsteps receding into the hum of the palace. Light caught the blue of her gown once more as she moved further down the hall.

Francis stood very still.

Tobie gave him a sidelong look. "Well," he murmured, "she was... refreshing."

Francis exhaled slowly. "Young," he said. "Very young."

"Yes," Tobie replied. "But did she see you or your new title?"

Francis didn't answer at first. The air felt changed, as though a new thread had been quietly woven into the tapestry of his life without his permission or awareness.

At last he said, "Let us go. I have had enough ceremony for one day."

They walked on.

Behind them, out of range of hearing, a young woman in a sky-blue gown paused to look back down the hall, as if she, too, sensed that something had just begun.

10

THE NEW WAY TO KNOW

Francis Bacon had read many books in his life, but writing one felt different. Like he wasn't just placing words on a page, he was placing stones along a path that would lead others to follow.

A path other people might one day walk. A path for discovering the truth. He sat hunched over his desk in the dim morning light, his quill hovering over a blank sheet that felt far too empty for the size of the idea in his head.

He whispered the words he'd been repeating for weeks: "A new way to know."

Saying it out loud made the idea feel bigger. Braver. Maybe a little dangerous. Saying it made goosebumps form on his arms.

From the fireplace, Tobie groaned without even lifting his eyes from the pile of letters he was sorting. "Start with a statement," he suggested wearily. "All good arguments start with a statement."

Francis tapped his quill. "My statement is that we've been learning wrong for centuries."

Tobie finally looked up. "If that's your statement, perhaps

add a few compliments around it. You know, soften the blow so Aristotle doesn't roll out of his grave and come fight you."

Francis considered that. "Yes… something gentler. Like 'The old ways are useful, but incomplete.'"

"That," Tobie said with a nod, "sounds like you'd like to stay alive."

Francis scribbled the line. He could feel the weight of the moment settling over him. This wasn't just another essay or legal opinion. Throughout his entire life, he'd been taught that the greatest truths came from old books, old thinkers, old rules.

But the idea that knowing can come from observation, from testing, by questioning, and recording careful details, had cracked open something inside him. The world wasn't a passage to memorize. It was a mystery to be investigated.

"How do I say that without insulting every scholar in England?" Francis muttered.

"Slowly," Tobie replied.

Two days later, the ink on the morning's correspondence had barely dried when Tobie Matthew stepped into Francis's study at Gray's Inn, brushing a bit of April rain from his cloak.

"You've caused a stir in the city," Tobie said lightly. "Every pamphleteer in London seems determined to report your doings before you've even done them."

Francis did not look up from the papers he was arranging. "If you refer to the wedding," he said with a faint smile, "I assure you it required no such attention."

Tobie raised a brow. "A quiet ceremony, then?"

"As quiet as anything can be when two families insist on formality," Francis replied. He paused, choosing his words with care, truthful, but neither sentimental nor dismissive. "Alice is… agreeable. Sensible. She carries herself well. We understand what is expected of us."

Tobie studied him. "And you are content?"

"Content," Francis repeated, as if tasting the word. "Yes. It is a practical arrangement. My work continues; her household is established. Nothing more is required."

A faint knock sounded in the hall, Alice's maid delivering a small parcel, no doubt something domestic. Francis accepted it without ceremony, setting it neatly aside on the table without opening it.

Tobie's smile was gentle but knowing. "Life moves forward, then."

"As it always must," Francis replied. He gathered a stack of notes—research for The Advancement of Learning, diagrams of method, ideas that still glowed with possibility. "Marriage is... one part of the whole, no more significant than any other necessity. My greater labors remain unchanged."

Tobie nodded. "Then may the union bring stability, at least."

"Stability," Francis said softly. "That is all I require."

Outside, the rain continued its quiet descent, drumming a rhythm steady and unremarkable.

A wedding had taken place duly, properly, with the fanfare his bride had required.

And Francis Bacon, newly married, returned to his work. Francis decided that writing wasn't enough. He needed practice explaining his ideas, and there was no better audience than the students of Gray's Inn.

They were skeptical of everything. Perfect.

He convinced a handful of them — some curious, some bribed with the promise of fresh bread — to meet him in the Inn's garden. When they arrived, frost dusted the grass, and their breath puffed white in the cold air.

Francis placed three objects on a stone bench: a feather, a small stone, and a scrap of cloth.

"Tell me," Francis announced, "which will fall fastest if I drop them?"

"The stone," several students said.

"Obviously," added a particularly bright student named Alan Turing.

Francis winced at the word. "Obviously" was to him what "stale bread" was to Tobie — always suspicious.

He climbed onto a low wall despite Tobie's whispering, "Francis, be careful."

Holding the feather and the stone, he called, "Prediction?"

"The stone!" came the chorus.

Francis released both.

The stone thumped onto the ground instantly.

The feather fluttered dreamily down as if it had all the time in the world.

The students smirked. "We told you."

Francis retrieved the objects. "Why did the stone fall faster?"

"It's heavier," one said confidently.

"Or," Francis countered, lifting the feather again, "because the feather must fight the air."

The students blinked.

Tobie added helpfully, "He means air resistance."

Francis picked up two stones, one large, one small, clearly of the same material.

"Now what?" he asked.

"They'll fall the same," said a younger boy.

"No, the heavier one will hit first." Alan objected.

Francis smiled. "How can we know?"

He released the stones. They struck the ground nearly together. A ripple of murmurs spread through the group.

"This," Francis said, holding up the stones, "is why we test. We don't assume. We observe. We ask questions. We experiment. That is the new method."

A curious and clever student raised his hand timidly. "But Aristotle said…"

"Yes," Francis said gently. "Aristotle observed brilliantly. But even a brilliant observer can be wrong. Or incomplete."

The boy nodded thoughtfully.

Francis saw something sparking behind his eyes, the same spark he'd felt thinking of the new method. It was curiosity that led to courage.

Back inside, Francis warmed his hands by the fire and stared at his half-finished manuscript. The pages beside him were filled with diagrams, notes, and metaphors he'd jotted at random hours of the night.

He dipped his quill and wrote: If a child may test water, earth, air, and flame, why should a scholar refuse the same?

He sat back, pleased.

Tobie, reading over his shoulder, nodded. "Bold. But polite."

"That is the goal," Francis said. "Boldness with manners."

"You're good at the first," Tobie said. "We're working on the second."

Francis smirked.

By spring, Francis's treatise, The Advancement of Learning, was ready for printing. At the press shop, the air smelled of hot metal and ink. The printer, Master Billings, squinted at Francis's manuscript.

"So this is… what? A guidebook to thinking properly?"

"A guidebook to discovering truth," Francis corrected.

Billings shrugged. "Truth is a tricky thing to sell."

But when the first copy slid from the press — warm, crisp, beautifully set — Francis felt a burst of pride so sharp it nearly hurt.

He held it reverently. "Tobie… we did it."

Tobie held another copy upside down. "Indeed. Very book-like."

The reaction arrived quickly. Students admired it. Young thinkers devoured it. Some scholars praised its clarity.

Others muttered in taverns: "Bacon thinks he can rewrite nature."

One particularly offended professor declared, "Bacon is like a child overturning furniture, just to see what's underneath!"

Francis, when Tobie repeated this, said, "Yes. That's precisely the point."

Tobie sighed. "You're impossible."

But despite resistance, his ideas spread faster than gossip after a feast.

Students visited him with eager questions. Apprentices asked how to build experiments. Even a timid stableboy wandered in one afternoon.

"Master Bacon, sir," he stammered, "is it true even someone like me can test ideas?"

Francis beamed. "Especially someone like you."

Tobie elbowed him. "He means that kindly."

Later that year, Francis held a demonstration for any Gray's Inn student brave enough to attend.

He set a candle on the long table in the dining hall.

"Step one," he said, "is observation. What do you see?"

"A flame," someone said.

"Light," said another.

"Heat," said a third.

Francis nodded. "Good. But what else?"

The room hesitated.

Tobie stage-whispered, "He wants details."

Francis pointed at the flame. "It moves when I move my

hand. Its smoke twists upward. It shrinks when I lower this shield."

He held a parchment next to the flame. It bent away.

"Step two: Ask a question. For example, 'Why does heat rise?'"

A young man raised his hand. "Because warm air weighs less?"

Francis lit up like a second candle. "Yes!"

"Step three: Test," he said. "Step four: Record your results truthfully."

He looked at them all. "Especially if the results surprise you."

Tobie muttered, "He says that from experience."

Francis ignored him.

"This is the method," he declared. "Not magic. Not memorization. Curiosity with structure."

As he spoke, the students leaned forward. Not because he was their teacher — he wasn't — but because they could feel something shifting. A door cracking open.

One night, after the students had left, and the candles burned low, Francis sat alone at his desk, turning a fresh copy of his book in his hands. He whispered to it.

"You are small. But perhaps... you will grow."

He imagined a world centuries ahead, where learning wasn't about obedience but questions. Where classrooms used experiments instead of fear. Where truth was built, tested, and shared.

Tobie slipped in quietly and saw the soft smile Francis wore. "You're staring at that book like it's a newborn child."

"In a way," Francis said, "it is."

Tobie sat beside him. "Do you think people will listen?"

Francis considered this.

"Yes," he said. "Not all. Not at once. But some will. Enough will."

He closed the book gently.

"This," Francis whispered, "is only the beginning."

Tobie smirked. "Of progress... or trouble?"

Francis grinned. "Both."

By autumn, The Advancement of Learning had traveled across England and beyond. Merchants carried copies in their wagons to France and Holland. Students smuggled them under their cloaks into lecture halls. A copy even made its way back to Italy, where this type of Renaissance thinking had begun.

Europe didn't know it yet, but Francis Bacon had planted a seed. Ideas, he realized, were like plants: water them with curiosity, give them sunlight through questions, and they spread. Wildly.

That night, Francis opened his oldest notebook, the one labeled Things That Don't Make Sense. On a blank page, he wrote: Today, something does make sense. The method works, and the world may one day understand it. He set his quill down.

Somewhere in the heart of Gray's Inn, in that hidden room he had claimed as his laboratory, a lonely lens caught a ray of moonlight and glimmered faintly, almost as if it agreed.

11

"THE CHANCELLOR'S CHAIR"

Becoming Lord Chancellor of England was not how Francis Bacon imagined it would feel.

He had pictured triumph, applause, admiration, the satisfaction of stepping into the most powerful legal office in the kingdom. A seat beside the King. Influence woven into every decision that shaped England's future.

Instead, on the morning of his appointment, Francis mostly felt... dizzy.

The chancellor's robes were heavy. Very heavy. They hung on him like an overloaded cloak of achievement, ambition, and the faint fear that everyone in the palace could see his knees shaking.

He stood at the window of his new chamber, staring out across Westminster. Fog rolled over the Thames, prowling through the city he was now sworn to help govern.

Tobie used to say politics was like the weather: unpredictable and guaranteed to ruin your plans when you least expected it.

Francis never understood the comparison until now.

King James was in especially exuberant form when Francis

went to thank him. James always enjoyed intellectual company, but today he seemed delighted, almost giddy.

"My dear Bacon!" the King exclaimed, clapping him on the shoulder so hard Francis nearly toppled. "England has ne'er had a Chancellor wi' a mind like yours. We shall be a nation o' wisdom."Francis bowed. "Your Majesty honors me. I will serve faithfully, and rationally."

James beamed. "Aye, aye, rationally! Reason! Order! Learnin'! No' like the last fellow—aye, always sulkin'. And Coke —och, dinna get me started on Coke."

Francis hid his smile. Sir Edward Coke was many things — brilliant, venomous, stubborn as a mule — but he was never boring.

"He disapproves o' everything I enjoy," James muttered. "Books, conversation, bonnie courtiers—absolutely nae appreciation for the finer things. But you! You appreciate inquiry. You're near a whole library in human form!"

Francis bowed again, mostly to hide his face.

As he left the royal chamber, he wondered briefly, selfishly, if perhaps finally his ideas about learning and evidence and reform might matter to the world.

When he arrived at the Court of Chancery for his first day presiding, reality hit him like a bucket of cold water.

Politics did not work the way experiments did.

The courtroom buzzed like an injured beehive. Petitioners pressed against each other, waving papers like desperate birds flapping their wings. Lawyers argued before Francis had even taken his seat. Clerks darted back and forth carrying bundles of parchment tied with string.

Francis tried to impose order.

"Let us proceed calmly," he said, raising a hand. No one listened.

He cleared his throat louder. "Gentlemen, please", Still nothing.

Finally, he stood, lifted the Chancellor's staff, and thumped it once against the floor. The hall went silent.

"Thank you," Francis said, relieved. "Now, let us hear the first case. In an orderly fashion." He called the parties forward. Before he could speak a single sentence, both lawyers exploded into accusations at once.

"He stole my client's property!"

"He forged the contract!"

"He lied at the last hearing!"

"He lies now!"

Francis blinked. "Did either of you bring evidence?"

They stared as though the concept was new.

"Evidence?" one lawyer echoed. "Facts?" The other said, slightly horrified.

Francis sighed. "Yes. Evidence. Facts. Proof. The basis of judgment. The foundation of truth."

Whispers rippled through the audience. Someone muttered, "Francis Bacon and his facts again."

Francis massaged his temples. He had learned things as a child, things the world seemed determined to forget. That truth needed testing, that claims required checking, that decisions should rely on information rather than noise.

Politics, he was learning, preferred noise.

He judged the first case. Then the second. Then fifteen more. He settled land disputes, family arguments, inheritance tangles, property complaints, and one exceptionally ugly quarrel about who owned a goose. At midday, he was exhausted.

Court proceedings felt like trying to conduct an orchestra where half the musicians were playing the wrong song and the other half hadn't tuned their instruments.

This, he thought ruefully, is not a system. It's chaos.

By late afternoon, Francis returned to his chamber. He had no sooner collapsed into his chair than a voice drawled from the doorway.

"Well, look who's wearing the Chancellor's robes."

Francis looked up.

Sir Edward Coke leaned in the doorway with the expression of a cat surveying a mouse who had just walked into a room filled with cats.

Coke's smile was coy, with no sincerity. "Congratulations, Francis."

"Thank you," Francis said evenly.

Coke stepped inside, hands clasped behind his back. "Quite a burden, that office. Requires discipline. Judgment. Tradition." He paused. "Qualities you... only dabble in."

Francis ignored the jab. "What do you want, Edward?"

"Oh, nothing," Coke said lightly. "Only to see how the great reformer manages the most ancient office in England."

Francis took a slow breath. "I intend to improve efficiency. Reduce delays. Base decisions on evidence rather than reputation."

Coke's eyebrows climbed so high they nearly left his face. "Evidence?" he repeated, as though Francis had proposed balancing the legal code on a dainty cup.

"Evidence," Francis confirmed.

Coke tilted his head. "You think you can turn the English courts into your laboratory?" His tone sharpened. "You think governance is an experiment?"

Francis met his glare. "All systems can be improved, Edward. Even this one. Especially this one."

Coke's voice went icy. "Careful, Francis. The higher you climb, the further you fall."

Francis felt a chill. But he did not flinch.

His adversary had a face.

And it was standing in his doorway.

Weeks passed. Then months. Francis rose early, worked late, and tried desperately to repair the court's broken machinery.

He created new rules for petitions. Shortened delays. Required written summaries and evidence. He introduced a system to track cases so none would be forgotten in dusty stacks of parchment. He refused lavish gifts. He refused secret influence.

He refused to play the same old game.

And the players of the old game hated him.

Whispers grew in corners of Westminster the way mold grows in damp wood, quietly, then everywhere at once.

"He is too proud."

"He thinks he knows better than everyone else."

"He questions traditions."

"He moves too fast."

"He talks of evidence like a scholar, not a statesman."

Francis could feel it, politics shifting beneath him like ice cracking on a river.

Even King James grew unpredictable. Some days he praised Francis's efficiency. On other days, he snapped at him for interfering with the whims of royal favorites, particularly George Villiers, the handsome young Duke of Buckingham, who seemed to glide through the palace on charm alone.

Buckingham liked Francis. When it suited him. He also liked replacing anyone who became more trusted than he was. Francis began to worry. But he kept working. He had to. If he could reform the courts, create rules that outlasted kings, then perhaps, finally, England would learn to think the way nature taught: through order, not chaos; through testing, not assumption.

One evening, after an especially difficult session, Francis sat in his chambers reading a petition. A candle flickered at his elbow, its light trembling with each draft that sneaked through the window.

A clerk entered quietly. "My lord... there are more complaints."

Francis rubbed his eyes. "About what?"

The clerk hesitated. "Your reforms."

Francis managed a tired smile. "Of course."

"People say you are overreaching," the clerk whispered. "That you deny the privileges of those who have always had influence. That you are arrogant."

Francis closed the petition carefully. "Truth," he said, "is often mistaken for arrogance."

The clerk looked uneasy. "Sir Edward Coke has been speaking publicly."

"Against me?"

The clerk nodded.

"And the King?"

"Silent, my lord."

Francis felt the pressure building. Thick, dark, and close. He opened his notebook — the same habit he'd carried from boyhood — and wrote: *Systems resist change. But if we cannot improve the laws of society, then what are we studying law for?*

He tapped the quill against the page.

Still, a man must know when the wind is shifting. The candlelight trembled again, as though shivering in agreement.

Winter settled over London like a wool blanket dipped in ice. Snow rimed the rooftops. The river narrowed under frost. But inside the palace, political heat intensified. Buckingham whispered to the King. Coke whispered in the halls. Enemies whispered everywhere. And Francis, despite his brilliance, could not hear every whisper.

One morning, a messenger arrived in Francis's chamber with a sealed letter, thick wax, royal crest, heavy with the weight of bad news. Francis broke the seal.

The words hit him like a blow: accusations, complaints, inquiries into his conduct. Not into his judgments, but into his acceptance of gifts — gifts common to the office, gifts he received years before becoming Chancellor, gifts every official took.

But now they were called something else. Bribes.

Francis closed his eyes. He thought of Essex, bold, reckless Essex, who ignored warnings until the world collapsed around him. He thought of Anthony, steady, loyal Anthony, who always told him to tread lightly. He thought of every experiment he had ever done, every law he had studied, every truth he had sought. Cause and effect.

He had tried to reform a system built on compromise and favoritism. And now, that system meant to swallow him whole. He stood slowly, robes heavy as chains. "Well," he whispered to the empty chamber, "then let us face the evidence."

But deep down, he already knew: The trial would not be about evidence. It would be about accusations. And accusation in politics was stronger than truth. The Chancellor's Chair loomed behind him, massive, ornate, unmoving. He touched it once, lightly. Then turned away.

12

THE GATHERING PRESSURE

Whitehall Palace smelled of wax and wet wool, winter lingering in the stones even as servants hurried to lay fresh rushes. Francis Bacon walked the familiar corridor alone, his new robes of office trailing behind him like a dark tide. The weight of the Lord Chancellor's chain still felt strange upon his shoulders, an honor and a burden fused into a single piece of gold.

A guard stepped aside and opened the door to the privy chamber.

King James sat by the hearth, boots extended toward the flames, a goblet of spiced wine in one hand and a sheaf of papers in the other. He looked up with a brightness that always seemed half theatrical, half sincere.

"Ah! My Lord Chancellor," he said, rolling the title across the room like a reward tossed to a favored hound. "Come, sit. I've a mind full o' smoke and need ye to clear it."

Francis bowed. "Your Majesty is kind to summon me."

"Kind? Nonsense," James waved him forward. "I need that great brain o' yours as much as England does. Sit, man."

Francis obeyed, settling into the high-backed chair opposite the King. For a moment, neither spoke, the fire crackling between them like an impatient third participant.

"Tell me, Francis, how fare your reforms? I hear ye are reducin' cases faster than a Scotsman spendin' English gold."

Francis allowed himself a quiet smile. "I have cleared more than two thousand cases since taking office. The courts run more efficiently now. Justice delayed is justice denied, after all."

"Aye," James said, sipping his wine. "But efficiency begets enemies. And I hear those enemies sharpenin' their claws."

Francis met the King's gaze. "Reform often bruises those who benefitted from disorder."

"Bruises?" James barked a laugh. "Ye've done more than bruise them; ye've taken food aff their table. Some men make their livin' on confusion."

"Then they should find more honorable employment," Francis said calmly.

James tilted his head, studying him. "Such a clean conscience ye have. Almost painful to look at. Reminds me o' sunlight glarin' aff snow."

Francis clasped his hands. "My goal, Majesty, is simple: a system governed by evidence, not influence."

James snorted. "Evidence? Influence is the blood in this kingdom's veins. Take it away, and the whole body faints."

Francis held his ground. "If England is to thrive, truth must rule its courts."

For a moment, James's expression softened, something like admiration flickering behind the heavy lids.

"Aye," he murmured. "And that is why I placed the Seal in your hands. Not because ye are pliable, God knows ye're no', but because ye are right."

The King leaned back, lowering his voice. "But listen well, Francis. Ye tread upon auld bones. And auld bones break loudly."

Francis felt a chill unrelated to winter. "You refer to Sir Edward Coke."

James's mouth twisted. "Who else? That man would wrestle wi' the sun if he thought it violated precedent."

"Coke resents my appointment," Francis said. "He sees reform as an insult to his legacy."

"Resents?" James scoffed. "He hates ye wi' a zeal usually reserved for heretics. And he whispers to the Commons that ye wield power too boldly."

Francis exhaled. "Boldness is required, Majesty. Your courts must not stagnate."

"Boldness," James repeated, "can be mistaken for overreach. And overreach for corruption."

Francis looked up sharply. "Corruption?"

James raised a hand. "Not by me. Ye've served me faithfully. But rumors gather in this kingdom like fog. I want ye to be prepared."

Francis's voice lowered. "I take no bribes."

"I know that," James said firmly. "But the world does nae care what is true. It cares what is useful. And some would find it useful to see ye brought down."

The silence that followed was thick, a weight in the room greater even than the Chancellor's robes upon Francis's shoulders.

"Majesty," Francis said at last, "if I have your confidence, I can weather their slander."

James studied him with a long, searching look, then nodded once.

"Ye have my confidence," he said. "But hear me: even kings can be made to bend to strong winds."

Francis bowed his head. "I will serve with integrity until the last."

"That is what worries me," James murmured, almost too softly to hear. "Integrity leaves a man exposed."

The fire snapped loudly, sending a spiral of sparks up the chimney. Outside, wind scraped the palace walls, a low and gathering moan.

"Go on then, Francis. Continue your reforms. But keep your eyes open. And your enemies closer."

Francis rose. "I shall, Majesty."

"And Francis?" The King's voice halted him at the door. "Remember, laws aren't the only things that must be balanced. So must the tempers o' powerful men."

Francis bowed once more. When he stepped back into the corridor, the draft of cold air struck him like a warning. He pulled his robes tighter around him, but the chill lingered.

Somewhere, he knew, Coke was sharpening his accusations. And the blustering winds James had feared were no longer gathering. It had already begun.

13

"THE FALL"

Francis Bacon had always believed that truth behaved like a well-run court case: collect evidence, examine it fairly, weigh claims against facts, and then deliver judgment. He had not yet learned how rarely the world followed its own rules.

London in early spring smelled of damp stone and ink, two scents Francis normally found comforting. But today, those smells felt heavy, like a book someone had slammed shut on his fingers. A gray mist clung to the streets as he walked toward Westminster Hall, the enormous chamber where England held its most important trials.

And today, Francis was not attending as a judge. He was attending as the accused.

Tobie walked beside him, pale as chalk. "It's not fair," he muttered. "None of this is fair."

Fairness? Francis almost laughed. For months now, rumors had swirled through court corridors like dust in a shaft of light, quiet at first, then louder, then impossible to ignore.

"Gifts," people whispered.

"Payments."

"Bribes."

Francis had accepted gifts, yes. Everyone in the government did. It was a tradition left over from medieval days when officials were paid in everything except actual salary. A turkey from one petitioner, a pouch of coins from another, a fancy piece of plate from a grateful nobleman. It was how the system worked.

But now the system had turned on him.

The mist gathered thicker as Westminster Hall loomed ahead, its high wooden ceiling like the ribs of a great beached whale. Francis stopped at the entrance. A hundred memories of the place rushed back: arguing cases, dazzling the gallery with logic, exposing contradictions, rescuing the weak with well-timed reasoning.

Today, those same skills felt useless.

"Francis," Tobie said softly, touching his arm. "You don't have to face this alone."

"Yes," Francis said. "I do."

The doors creaked open.

Inside, rivals waited.

Edward Coke stood like a dark pillar among them, his eyes bright with cold satisfaction. Coke had fought Francis for years over legal ideas, royal favor, even who received credit in speeches. He had called Francis too imaginative for the law, too experimental for government, too clever for his own good.

Now he stood as part of the committee judging Francis's honor. Cause and effect, Francis thought bleakly. He had challenged Coke's authority years ago. Today's trial was the echo.

As Francis took his seat, murmurs rippled through the chamber.

"That's him, Lord Chancellor no more..."

"Used to be the clever one..."

"A shame."

"A scandal."

Francis kept his gaze steady. He would not shrink. A man of

evidence must face accusations the same way he faced experiments, with clarity, with calm, with courage.

The proceedings began. Lord Saye read the charges: that Francis Bacon, as Lord Chancellor, had accepted gifts from petitioners whose cases were before his court. That such gifts suggested improper influence. That such influence suggested corruption. Each charge struck like a hammer shaping metal.

Bacon lifted his chin. "My lords," he said, "I confess freely that I accepted gifts. But I deny absolutely that any gift swayed a judgment. I judged by the law alone."

Coke stepped forward, voice smooth as polished granite. "Intentions are irrelevant," he said. "Perception is what matters. When a judge accepts gifts, how is the public to separate truth from temptation? Integrity must be spotless."

Francis met his rival's eyes. "Spotless is not the same as lifeless, Sir Edward. If a judge is given a roasted goose at Christmas, shall he be accused of corruption by the poultry?"

A few lords snorted into their sleeves. Coke did not.

"The law," Coke said frostily, "is not a feast. And you have forgotten your place at the table."

Francis felt the words like arrows. He had built his life on logic, structure, reform, on the belief that human systems could be improved the same way natural ones could be understood. But Coke represented tradition — heavy as iron, rules older than fairness, customs older than reason.

And the chamber agreed with him.

Francis watched faces shift: some sympathetic, some stern, many scared. People were not weighing evidence; they were weighing danger. If they defended Bacon, they risked the King's disfavor. If they condemned him, they might be safe.

Fear, Francis realized, was always stronger than truth in politics. The Lord Treasurer read a letter from the King. "His Majesty hopes this matter will conclude without disturbance to the realm."

That sentence settled over Francis like a shroud. It meant: Do not rock the boat. Take the fall. Protect the crown.

Tobie leaned close. "Francis. You cannot accept blame for what you did not do."

Francis looked down at his hands, the hands that had written books, designed experiments, judged cases, built a career on precision.

"Tobie," he whispered, "if I fight this, the King's enemies will use it against him. The court will fracture. England will shake. The truth will not matter, only the appearance of scandal."

"So you would sacrifice yourself?" Tobie demanded.

Francis thought of Essex — bold, passionate Essex — destroyed by pride and refusal to bend. Francis had watched his friend's fall. He had sworn never to repeat it. But now he understood that sometimes bending was the only way to keep the world from cracking.

"My lords," he said, voice steady though his chest felt hollow, "I submit myself wholly to your judgment. A servant of the crown must sometimes bear more weight than is fair. I pray only that my years of service be remembered."

Gasps flickered across the chamber. Coke's lips tightened in victory.

Tobie grabbed his arm. "Francis... no."

Francis squeezed his friend's hand. "It is the only path that keeps the kingdom stable."

The committee retired. The whole hall buzzed like a hive struck with a stick.

Within an hour, they returned. Guilty of corruption. A heavy fine. Removal from office. Barred from public employment.

The words fell like stones into a well, each one sinking deeper than the last. Tobie's eyes filled with tears. "They have ruined you."

Francis shook his head gently. "Not ruined. Redirected."

But as he walked out of Westminster Hall, no longer Chancellor, no longer powerful, no longer needed, he felt a weight he had never felt before. Shame.

Not because he believed he was guilty, but because he had accepted guilt to protect a system that had failed to protect him.

Outside, the mist had lifted. The sunlight glinted off the Thames like shards of glass. Francis stopped at the edge of the water and watched the current pull fragments of light downstream.

Evidence and accusations, he thought. Two different things. In science, only evidence mattered. In politics, only accusations mattered.

He understood now, painfully, that his life had always been caught between those two worlds. And today, the wrong one had won.

Tobie touched his shoulder. "What will you do now?"

Francis breathed in the cold air, steadying himself. "What I have always done," he said. "Observe. Question. Learn."

He looked at the river, ever moving, ever changing. "And perhaps," he whispered, "begin again."

14

"SNOW, A CHICKEN, AND
A FINAL QUESTION"

Francis Bacon had never been good at staying still. Retirement — forced retirement — was supposed to quiet a man. It was supposed to tuck him away like an old book placed carefully on a high shelf. But Francis was not a book, and he refused to gather dust. His mind still whirred like a waterwheel after heavy rain, turning questions into motion.

He lived now at his country house, Gorhambury in Hertfordshire, a modest place tucked beside a narrow lane lined with elms. The air smelled of wood smoke and damp earth. It was peaceful. That in and of itself felt suspicious.

Most mornings he walked the grounds with his cloak pulled tight, notebook in hand, Anthony's memory still lingering at his side like a steady heartbeat. His brother's loss had left an empty place in his life. Francis felt now his life was full of empty places, and sometimes he would pause mid-stride as if listening for footsteps that no longer followed him.

But even grief could not silence curiosity.

He wrote constantly. Pages upon pages. Essays, theories, experiments, reflections. His handwriting had grown shakier over the years, but the ideas inside the lines crackled with the energy of a young boy staring at water rippling in a palace window.

The world may have taken his title, his office, his influence, but it had not taken his purpose.

It could not.

One late winter afternoon, Francis met his old friend, Dr. Rawley, at Highgate, a village perched like a watchtower on the northern edge of London. They had been arguing for an hour already, pleasantly, the way scholars argue when they respect each other too much to shout but not enough to agree.

Rawley pointed at the sky. "Snow again," he noted. "Be grateful we're inside."

Francis stood by the window, watching the flurries dance like tiny pale moths. "Snow is not an inconvenience," he murmured. "It is information."

Rawley groaned. "Everything is information to you."

"Everything is information," Francis corrected. "Nature writes her laws on the world. We need to learn only how to read them."

Rawley poured more ale. "You sound like you're about to invent another experiment."

Francis's eyes glimmered.

Rawley froze. "Francis... no."

"Yes," Francis said, already grabbing his cloak. "Come, we need a chicken."

"A what?"

"A chicken."

Rawley blinked. "For what purpose?"

"For science," Francis said simply.

Outside, the snow had thickened. It clung to hedges and rooftops, softening the village into white silence. Francis moved with surprising energy for an old man, his boots crunching through drifts as he crossed the yard toward a nearby cottage.

Rawley scrambled after him. "At least tell me what you intend to do before you frighten the farmers!"

"It's simple," Francis said. "I've been wondering whether cold can slow decay. If so, snow might preserve meat."

Rawley stared. "You mean to freeze... a chicken?"

Francis nodded. "Exactly."

Rawley sighed. "Only you," he muttered, "would turn a winter storm into a research opportunity."

They reached a small farmhouse where a woman was stuffing hay into the chicken coop. When Francis explained his request, she gave him a long, baffled look. Then, perhaps because she recognized him from his days of prominence—or perhaps because she was simply amused—she handed him a recently slaughtered bird wrapped in cloth.

Francis thanked her with the solemnity of a knight receiving a sacred relic.

Outside the cottage, the wind swirled flakes around them like white sparks. Francis knelt in the snow, brushing aside a patch of clean ground.

"Help me dig," he said.

Rawley sighed again, though the corners of his mouth twitched. "I should have stayed in bed today."

They dug a hollow, packed it with snow, placed the chicken inside, then covered it with another thick layer of icy powder until it resembled a misshapen white mound.

Francis clapped his hands. "There. A perfect trial."

Rawley eyed the frost clinging to Francis's beard. "A perfect way to die of cold, perhaps. Come inside before you freeze solid like your unfortunate bird."

Francis hesitated, studying the mound as if waiting for something miraculous to occur. But snow behaved like snow; it sat quietly, glittering under the dim, clouded light.

Rawley gently tugged his sleeve. "Francis. Inside."

Francis nodded and rose, brushing snow from his gloves. "Yes... yes, of course."

But as they walked back toward the house, Francis felt a sudden tightness in his chest, like invisible fingers squeezing the air from his lungs. He stopped mid-step.

Rawley turned. "Francis?"

Francis tried to wave him off, but his breath came in short, shallow bursts. The world blurred, whitened. Snowflakes stung his face like cold needles.

Not now, he thought. The experiment wasn't finished.

Rawley rushed to his side. "You're chilled through. We're going inside this instant."

Francis tried to protest but couldn't form the words. His legs gave way beneath him.

Rawley caught him under the arms and dragged him toward the house, shouting for help.

An hour later, Francis lay in the bed of the guest room, wrapped in blankets piled so high he felt like a quilted mountain. His body ached with a deep, trembling cold that refused to release him. The illness came swiftly, too swiftly. Pneumonia, likely. The price of curiosity was sometimes steeper than he wished to admit.

Rawley sat beside him, rubbing warmth into his hands. "You fool," he whispered, though his voice cracked. "You brilliant, impossible fool."

Francis forced a smile. "It was a good question."

"Not worth your life."

Francis's eyelids fluttered. The room blurred and sharpened in turn, like an image reflected on rippling water.

"It is always worth asking a question," he murmured. "Even the dangerous ones."

Rawley bowed his head. "Rest. You must rest."

But Francis's mind was still moving. Still circling the idea like a hawk riding a current of thought.

"The snow…" he whispered. "The chicken… If cold prevents decay, then perhaps food may be stored longer in winter. Perhaps cold itself is a tool." He paused for breath, his voice as thin as frost. "Imagine it, Rawley. Preservation not through salt alone, but through nature's own design."

Rawley's eyes shone with grief. "Francis. Be silent. Your lungs cannot bear this."

But Francis shook his head slightly, stubborn to the very edge. "I must say it while I can."

His breaths came slower now, each one a negotiation with his failing body.

"I began… long ago… by observing a raindrop," he said. "One raindrop on a palace window. I wondered why it moved as it did. Why nature never repeated herself exactly."Rawley nodded, tears slipping silently down his cheeks.

"And now," Francis whispered, "my last observation… will be snow."

He turned his face toward the frosted window. Outside, the storm had settled into a quiet drift, flakes spiraling down like soft ash from some distant celestial fire.

"Snow is cold truth," he murmured. "Unornamented. Uncompromising. It preserves… but it also erases. Prints, tracks, boundaries… all blurred. Perhaps that is why I liked it. It demands a new understanding.

Rawley squeezed his hand. "You gave the world new understanding."

Francis's breath hitched. "Not enough. Not yet."

"You've given it a method," Rawley said. "A way forward."

Francis exhaled slowly. "Yes… a ladder. Output: One step at a time. Observation… question… test… record… share." His lips curved faintly. "The world will climb it long after I am gone."

Rawley's voice broke. "Don't speak like that."

Francis closed his eyes. The ache in his chest pulsed like a heavy, rhythmic drum. But beneath the pain, he felt a strange warmth—not physical, but something deeper, steadier. Purpose.

"I have failed in many things," he whispered. "Politics... ambition... loyalty... Perhaps I misunderstood the court. Perhaps I misunderstood myself."

He opened his eyes again, gaze clear despite the haze of fever.

"But I did not misunderstand nature. She is honest. Even when she is cruel."

Rawley bowed his head. "Then let the world remember you for that."

Francis inhaled, shallow but calm. The snow outside thickened once more, soft flakes spiraling across the faded evening sky. Each one different. Each one perfect.

"Rawley..." he murmured.

"Yes, Francis?"

"There is one question... left."

Rawley leaned close. "What is it?"

Francis's fingers twitched weakly around his friend's hand. "When... will mankind finally learn... to trust... evidence?"

Rawley swallowed, unable to answer.

Francis blinked once, slowly, as though studying the shape of that last thought. "Someday," he whispered. "Someday."

His breath thinned.

Then stopped.

The candle beside the bed guttered, bowed, and went out.

In the morning, the storm lifted.

Rawley walked outside wrapped in a thick cloak. The world was hushed under a heavy blanket of snow, the chicken still buried in its icy tomb like a strange monument to curiosity.

He knelt, touched the surface. The snow glittered sharply in the pale light.

Softly, Rawley said, "You were right, Francis. Cold preserves."

He closed his eyes, letting the silence settle around him.

Then he whispered the words that would outlive them both: "Let us test. Let us observe. Let us learn."

And the world slowly, steadily, like snow melting into spring, began to do exactly that.

EPILOGUE

Epilogue: "Seeds Growing in the Dark,"

Four hundred years after Francis Bacon buried a chicken in the snow, a seventh-grade classroom hummed with the familiar chaos of controlled curiosity.

The room smelled faintly of pencil shavings, warm radiator pipes, and whatever mysterious substance the cafeteria called "Tuesday Special." Posters of planets and famous scientists lined the walls, and a paper clock above the door ticked loudly, reminding everyone that time waited for no one, not even middle schoolers.

At the front of the classroom stood Ms. Jefferson, sleeves rolled up, safety goggles perched on her head like a crown of fierce enthusiasm. She tapped the board with her marker.

TODAY'S EXPERIMENT:

Does temperature affect how fast-food spoils?

A few students gasped in mock horror.

Marcus raised his hand. "Ms. J, are you making us eat rotten food?"

"No," she said. "But your dramatic energy is appreciated."

Laughter rippled through the room.

Ms. Jefferson set three bowls on the front table — one with a grape, one with a slice of bread, and one with a small piece of chicken. All were perfectly fresh.

"You will not be tasting anything," she said firmly. "We are observing. Testing. Comparing. Using the scientific method."

At the back of the room, Jada whispered to her partner Sam, "This is because that guy Bacon froze a chicken, isn't it?

"Yes," Sam said, flipping through the class textbook. "He's the one who invented experiments."

"He didn't invent experiments," Jada corrected. "He just figured out the steps so people would stop arguing about facts without checking them first."

Sam frowned. "So he invented homework?"

"No," Jada said. "He invented science fair projects."

Sam groaned. "Even worse."

Up front, Ms. Jefferson held up a laminated page: a portrait of Sir Francis Bacon, looking regal, serious, and slightly annoyed, as though someone had just messed up one of his experiments.

"Four centuries ago," she said, "this man believed something radical: that knowledge should be built on evidence, not assumptions. He spent his life asking questions, designing experiments, and taking notes. Many people doubted him. Some mocked him. Some feared him."

She paused, looking around at her students.

"But he kept asking questions anyway. Even when it cost him everything."

The class quieted. Marcus raised his hand again. "So... we're doing this experiment because of him?"

"In a way, yes," Ms. Jefferson said. "Today we test a question Bacon wondered himself: Does cold slow decay? He didn't have refrigerators, or thermometers, or sterile gloves. He had snow. And curiosity."

She gestured toward the three stations set up around the room.

STATION A: Room temperature
STATION B: Mini refrigerator
STATION C: Heat lamp

"You will place identical samples of food at each station," she explained. "You will observe them throughout the week. You will record differences. You will compare results."

Sam raised his hand. "What happens if one of them gets really gross?"

"Then," Ms. Jefferson said, "you have collected excellent data."

Jada made a face. "Do we have to smell it?"

"No, absolutely not."

Students formed groups, each carrying notebooks already crammed with doodles, diagrams, and half-finished equations. Some wrote with intense precision. Others wrote as if their pencils were trying to escape. All of them, though, cared more than they would ever admit.

At Station A, Marcus bent over the sample. "Room temperature," he read, tapping his chin. "So this one's like regular life."

"Boring life," added Zoe.

At Station B, Sam placed his grape in the fridge next to someone else's chicken. "This feels weird," he whispered. "Like we're giving it a tiny hotel room."

"Yeah," Jada said. "Five-star freezing."

At Station C, under the heat lamp, Miguel winced. "This is definitely going to rot first."

"But we can't say that yet," his partner reminded him. "We have to test it. Bacon rules."

"Right," Miguel said. "Evidence before assumptions."

Around the room, goggles fogged, pencils scratched, and the spirit of inquiry settled like a warm, bright light. It felt—unexpectedly—exciting.

Ms. Jefferson wandered from station to station, asking questions Bacon himself would have loved: "What do you observe? What changes over time? How do you know your conclusion is correct? What could affect your results?"

The students answered with growing confidence.

By the end of class, samples were labeled, placed in their correct stations, and sealed in clear containers like tiny edible time capsules. The bell rang. Chairs scraped. Backpacks zipped. A few students stayed behind, drawn to something they couldn't name.

Jada approached the front table. "Ms. R? Did Bacon ever... regret stuff? Because the textbook said he had a rough ending."

Ms. Jefferson smiled gently. "I think he regretted politics. But not science."

"Why?"

"Because he believed questions matter—even when the answers don't come easily. Even when they make people uncomfortable. Even when they change everything."

Jada nodded slowly, as though tucking that thought somewhere important.

Marcus lingered too. "Do you think he ever knew how much he changed the world?"

Ms. Jefferson looked at the notebook on her desk, the front page decorated with a student's messy drawing of the scientific method as a staircase.

"I think," she said softly, "that he trusted someone in the future would keep asking questions. That was enough."

As the last students slipped out, the room fell quiet.

Three small containers sat on the front table, waiting, slowly changing, teaching in silence.

Ms. Jefferson looked at the portrait of Bacon again. "You'd like this lesson," she whispered. "Especially the part about the chicken."

Outside, dusk settled over the school grounds. Windows glowed warmly against the fading sky. Inside one of those rooms, tucked away on a shelf where the lights never quite reached, sat a binder labeled: SCIENCE FAIR — IDEAS TO TEST.

Inside it were dozens of proposals, sketches, hypotheses, seeds of curiosity waiting in the dark.

Waiting to grow.

Because somewhere in the heart of every question, no matter how small, lived the same spark that once guided a young boy watching a raindrop slide down a palace windowpane.

A spark that said:
  Observe.
  Question.
  Test.
  Learn.
  Share.
  A spark that never truly went out.

ACKNOWLEDGMENTS

Sally Gibbins: Thank you for your expertise and for the genuine heart you put into your work. I've so appreciated your support and collaborative spirit. Checking the historical accuracy was a crucial step, and your contributions have truly made this story shine.

Jo Armitage: The best editor. Thank you for your time and talent. Your excitement about learning about the lives of old scientists is encouraging and drives me to work harder.

Chloe Maey: Many thanks for letting me use you as a sounding board and for talking through plot issues. I do appreciate your silly Bacon puns.

Melissa LeFevre: Thank you for reading and providing your historical lens.

Sara Runyan: Thank you for reading, dissecting, and letting me borrow your analytical brain.

Author's Note

A New Way to Know is not a conventional biography of Francis Bacon. It is a character-driven historical novel that traces how a curious child, shaped by courtly power, personal loss, friendship, and moral compromise, slowly becomes the thinker who would help redefine how humanity seeks truth.

Writing Bacon required holding two truths at once: that he was a foundational figure in the development of modern empirical thinking, and that he was also deeply human, ambitious, vulnerable, loyal, conflicted, and often wounded by the very systems he served. This novel focuses less on the polished philosopher and more on the formation of the mind behind the ideas.

Bacon's philosophy did not emerge fully formed. It grew from questions, small, persistent questions. about what books claimed and what the world revealed. To capture this, I grounded his early years in historically accurate settings such as Gray's Inn, Elizabethan court life, and Renaissance educational practices, while imagining the private experiments, notebooks, and internal struggles that history leaves unrecorded.

The "method" that would later shape science is presented here not as an abstract system, but as a survival skill: a way for Bacon to anchor himself to truth when tradition failed, authority contradicted observation, and emotion threatened to overwhelm reason.

Elizabethan England was a world where advancement depended on favor, not merit alone. Bacon's relationship with Robert Devereux, Earl of Essex, stands at the emotional and ethical core of this novel. Their friendship — brilliant, volatile, and ultimately tragic — illustrates the danger of unchecked passion and the price of loyalty in a political system that demanded obedience over affection.

The Essex rebellion and trial are drawn from historical record, but the emotional weight of Bacon's testimony, the cost of choosing truth over friendship, is explored imaginatively, with respect for documented events and their known consequences.

Equally formative were the losses that shaped Bacon: the death of his father, the crushing reality of inheritance laws, and, most profoundly, the loss of his brother Anthony. These moments stripped away certainty and forced Bacon to confront a world where brilliance did not guarantee security, and truth did not guarantee comfort.

In this novel, grief is not incidental. It is catalytic. It hardens resolve, sharpens thinking, and pushes Bacon toward a vision of knowledge that could endure when people, power, and favor could not.

While major events, figures, and institutions are rooted in historical scholarship, dialogue, inner thoughts, and some minor characters have been imagined, giving emotional continuity to the record.

If this story succeeds, it is not because it explains Bacon's ideas, but because it shows why he needed them.

Because sometimes a new way to know is not born from certainty, but from grief, doubt, and the refusal to stop asking questions.

Sincerely, Jeremy D. Scholz

BIBLIOGRAPHY

BIOGRAPHIES AND GENERAL HISTORY

BBC Bitesize. "Elizabeth I's government: Revision 3." Accessed 2025.

Brain, J. (2022). "Francis Bacon." *Historic UK.*

Lea, K. M. (2025). "Francis Bacon, Viscount Saint Alban." *Encyclopædia Britannica.*

National Museums Scotland. "A brief history of James VI and I."

Simpson, D. "Francis Bacon." *Internet Encyclopedia of Philosophy.*

Legal and Academic Studies

McCabe, B. (1964). "Francis Bacon and the Natural Law Tradition." *Natural Law Forum,* 9, 111–121.

Pirie, M. (2021). "Francis Bacon Imprisoned." *Adam Smith Institute.*

Scientific and Literary Contributions

Dawkins, P. (2020). "Francis Bacon, Shakespeare & the Earl of Essex." *Francis Bacon Research Trust.* **Edward Worth Library.** "Francis Bacon and the Advancement of Learning."

IOP Education. "Bacon's Fatal Experiment." *IOPSpark.*

Princeton University Library. "Francis Bacon."

Regional and Family History

Gerald, L. (1997). "Gorhambury, the Bacon Family and the Eight Shakespeare Quartos."

SirBacon.org. "Sir Francis Bacon's New Advancement of Learning."